Tattered Allegiance

Tattered Allegiance

MM FANTASY ROMANCE

A LUMINIA NOVEL

LEE COLGIN

<h1 style="text-align:center">About This Novel</h1>

Turmoil is brewing in the southern lands. Hushed voices whisper of war. When humans revolt against Fae authority, which perilous path will a young mixling choose?

Rahz

I love Jindal with all my heart, but he's full fae, and I'm only a mixling. He doesn't grasp how much harder life is for me. As the chasm yawns between us, I'm afraid we'll lose everything we've built.

Jindal

Rahz is my world, and whether he believes it or not, I'd do anything for him. Even when we struggle, my fealty is true. And so is my love. I refuse to let anything tear us apart.

Danger arrives in a royal carriage, gilded with jewels and trailing colorful silks. A loathsome pledge. A demanded oath. A cursed registry.

Can Rahz and Jindal weather the oncoming storm, or will a tattered allegiance break their vows and shatter their hearts?

Tattered Allegiance is the first book in Lee Colgin's new Luminia Series. Surrender to an enchanting tale of friends-to-lovers romance. Immerse yourself in Rahz and Jindal's fantasy world full of apricot pastries, mischievous bullies, young crushes, mysterious gatekeeping bogeymen, and lots of spicy times in the hayloft. A steamy MM paranormal love story in which being queer is normal and accepted, being a bully is uncalled for, and being childhood sweethearts is one in a million!

Chapter One

RAHZ

I STALK INTO THE FOREST THAT SURROUNDS OUR village, fists clenched so tightly my nails bite into my palms, but even the sting can't take the edge off my bruised feelings. Jindal had no reason to side with the others against me. Just because he's full fae and I'm only half doesn't make him better. I don't care what the rest of them think, but Jindal *knows* me. And he should have had my back.

The dense underbrush—purple vines, sweet-smelling blue honeypods, and a thorny rope of dandyrose—slows me down. I plow over them like royalty over peasants, without care for what lies beneath me. The flowers have the nerve to waft their cloying aroma skyward, even as I stamp them under my boots.

"Stupid history lesson," I mutter to myself, knowing I'm being childish and hating myself for it. I'm thirteen, nearly grown, but today's teasing has gotten under my skin. "Stupid test. Stupid Jindal." I don't need any of them. My mother will believe me when I tell her I didn't cheat.

"Hey, Rahz!" Jindal's high-pitched voice flies through the trees, followed by the faerie himself. Stupid wings, I add to my list. I don't have wings of my own, not even the stubby, flightless kind most mixlings possess, and especially not an impressive pair of working beauties like the ones Jindal sports on his slender back. "Wait up!"

I break into a run, crunching twigs and last season's leaves beneath my slamming footsteps. Jindal is the last person I want to talk to right now. Traitor.

"Rahz, please." If his voice holds a hint of remorse, I ignore it. "I'm sorry, okay?"

He can shove his worthless apology right up a nillyslug's arse for all I care. If he was really sorry, he wouldn't have betrayed me in the first place.

Jindal catches up easily enough. Even dodging brush and branch, he'll always be faster than me. Flying is faster than running. He drops straight into my path, and I plow into him.

We crash to the ground with a *whump*, me on top. Jindal lies flat on his back, wings trapped uselessly underneath him. Serves him right. Not that he minds, if his grin is any indication.

Stupid grin.

"Sorry, sorry," he chatters, seemingly unharmed. "Are you okay?"

I roll off him. My palms are scraped, and my wrists throb, having borne the brunt of the impact in an effort not to crush him beneath me in the fall. "Fine. No thanks to you." On my back, I gaze at the bright afternoon sky in its cloudless lavender glory. My eyes have gone watery, but I refuse to cry.

"Don't be mad." Jindal flops over me, pinning me to the cool earth with half his body weight concentrated on the boney point of one elbow that digs into my gut painfully.

I groan and shove him off.

"How was I supposed to know you didn't cheat?" He stares down at me, brows drawn, orange eyes glittering.

"Because you're my friend." I turn away, sit up, and brush the dirt off my clothes. The image of Jindal standing with the other faeries instead of me flickers through my mind. "Or you *were*."

"I *am*. But what's that got to do with cheating?"

I blink and drag my hands over my face. "I'm not that sort of person. I don't lie."

"Of course you don't, but no one passed except you. The test wasn't fair. There were questions we'd never discussed. How did you know the answers?"

Mother's books, that's how, but should I tell Jindal that? He'll think I'm stuffy. Boring. Sitting at home reading while the others hang out without me. I hesitate long enough for Jindal to wave me off.

"Never mind. You're smart. I know that. I'm sorry I doubted you, but I didn't side with the others."

"You did."

"Rahz." He says my name like an admonishment.

I scowl and match his tone. "Jindal."

He grimaces. "My *assigned* seat is on the opposite side of the room from yours. I can't help if I'm in the middle of Vander's goons."

In my mind, I see him standing next to Vander and the others, and his argument doesn't quite ring true. Maybe he can't control where he sits, but he didn't have to chuckle along, he didn't have to nudge Vander in the ribs when he was goading me, and he didn't have to stay silent when there was no one else on my side.

Whatever. I shuffle to my feet, and Jindal follows. He doesn't stand close. A bit of lichen has lodged itself in his long plum curls, minty green against the dark purple hue. The urge to reach out and pluck it from the tangle rises and falls. Let him be messy. It's his fault we ended up on the ground anyway.

His stare burns my cheeks. "You're really upset about this, aren't you?"

I grind my teeth. Maybe I overreacted, but admitting as much, even to myself, only makes me feel worse.

"I'm sorry, Rahz. Truly." His voice softens. "I should've defended you. I see that now, but I didn't realize it at the time. Please don't be mad. You're my best friend."

The fire in my belly dwindles to sparks. He sounds like he means it, and I want to believe him.

He kicks at the dirt and doesn't quite make eye contact. "You're still coming to my round moon party, right?"

I huff out an irritated sigh and hunch my shoulders. I've always looked forward to our monthly round moon sleepovers, when Jindal's father leaves for the neighboring village and we have their whole cottage to ourselves. But I don't know if I want to come tonight, not after what happened at our lessons.

Embarrassment tightens my stomach and heats my neck. Besides, the others don't like me. Jindal is my only true friend, but maybe he'd have more fun if I wasn't there.

"Please," he says when I fail to answer. "You have to come. It won't be the same if you're not there. Plus, Bessa made your favorite apricot pastries."

My mouth waters thinking about the brown sugar, cinnamon, and apricot perfections that are Bessa's pastries. I could eat a whole dozen by myself. Two dozen if I skip supper.

"She'll be sad if you don't come and Vander gets them all."

Can't have that. The thought of Vander stuffing himself with my favorite treat boils my blood. Maybe I do want to be there tonight.

I press my lips into a tight line and sulk. Jindal creeps forward with cautious steps until he stands right in front of me. Our eyes meet. My ordinary green human shade and his ethereal orange fae irises lock and hold.

"Oh, come on, Rahz. I said I was sorry. I mean it. I know

you didn't cheat, and don't worry about the others. They've probably already forgotten the whole thing. And no one's going to be thinking about lessons when we have games to play, sweets to eat, and scary stories to tell." He peers up at me through fluttering lashes. Does he know that turns my brain to mush?

My resolve wavers. I love scary stories, and I memorized a good one for tonight. One about the Gatekeeper I read in my mother's books. I want to tell it. I want to scare Vander. "All right. Fine. I'll be there."

More lash-fluttering. "And?"

I cross my arms. "And what?"

"Am I forgiven?" A hopeful look lights his eyes to a warm peach glow.

I can't stay mad at Jindal for long. "Fine. You're forgiven." I pluck the lichen from his hair and toss it aside. His grin leaves me breathless as he returns the favor, brushing fingers through my silver tresses to rid them of twigs and pine needles.

"I'll walk you home," he offers.

"No, thanks." I need some time alone. Time to let the anger seep out. Because even though it's the truth when I say I forgive him, the hurt at being accused of something I wouldn't do lingers. "I'll see you tonight."

Jindal's wings flap into motion, sending a pleasant breeze that cools my neck and ruffles my hair. He lifts off the ground to hover in place. "See you tonight. And I'll never let the others talk bad about you again. Promise."

Must be nice to have wings, I think, staring after him as he flies away. I watch until he's a sparkling pink and purple speck in the distance and mutter to myself, "Don't make promises you can't keep."

Chapter Two

Jindal

"Bye, Father." I stand on the threshold of our front door, picking at the splintered wood around the frame. The sun hangs low in the sky, casting a bronze glow over the grassy fields and shadowing my father in silhouette.

He turns his horse and faces me. I can't see his expression, but I'd bet my snail shell collection it's grim. "Behave." His voice is stern, as usual. "Keep everyone in line, unlike last time. I expect a glowing report from Bessa when I get home, and that's what I'd better get."

A frazzle of nerves rips through me, making my belly queasy. Last round moon, Vander had the brilliant idea to terrorize the neighbors' goats. If you scare them badly enough, they faint, which Vander thinks is hilarious. I think it's mean. What did the goats ever do to him?

The neighbors hadn't been pleased, and they'd said as much to my father. My punishment was to eat nothing but mash for supper for two weeks, which is torture enough, but it's even harder when the savory aroma of Bessa's cooking wafts from the kitchen every evening. The last thing I want is a repeat of that experience, but knowing my father, I can predict the next punishment to be something worse. Best not to get into trouble at all.

"We'll be good, sir." My voice breaks embarrassingly, and I cough to clear it. "No need to worry."

At that, he leaves without a backward glance for whatever he does every round moon at Clodhill, the next village over. I'm pretty sure he has a girlfriend over there, but I know better than to ask. Who knows what he'd do if he thought I was being nosy?

My mother went dormant when I was a newborn, and it's been just me and Father ever since. And though many fae would stay true to a dormant mate as they slept, I don't think my father is one of them. Not that I mind. I've never met Mother—though I often visit her swaddled sleeping form at the temple where she rests—and I enjoy the time when he's away too much to fret over the details. The house is less stifling with him gone.

I could feel sorry for myself. Sometimes I do. No mother. A harsh father. But mostly I'm glad I *have* a father, even if he doesn't like me all that much. Fae babies who lose both parents to dormancy are rumored to be claimed by the Gatekeeper. I repress a shiver. Any fate is better than that.

The dull but ever-present yearning stirs in my belly. Will Mother ever wake? What is she like? Is her skin a pale pink like mine, or does hers have the olive luster of Father's? He refuses to speak of her, so I'm left to wonder and to hold open a space in my heart for her when she wakes. With any luck, I'll find out sooner than later, but dormancy is unpredictable. Some fae sleep only a handful of seasons, while others drowse on for hundreds of cycles. Such is the price of near immortality.

Dwelling on her used to make me miserable. Tears flowed easily when I was little and didn't know better than to let my emotions show. But as the years pass, the melancholy has numbed to a dull ache, and even when I let myself wallow, the sadness isn't so bad anymore.

I have Bessa, our maid, to cheer me up. She's human and knows all the best recipes. She's smart and kind and somehow navigates Father's bad temper better than I do. I owe her for getting me out of one disaster after another. Bessa is the closest thing I have to a mother until mine wakes up, and I love her.

And I have Rahz, my best friend, even if he is mad at me half the time lately. I'm not sure what I've done to land so thoroughly on his bad side. Not that he really has one. Rahz might growl and bark at me, but he'd never bite. He's gentle at heart. The others pick on him, but it's just to see what he'll do. He's bigger than us, a half human mixling and all muscle. His skin reddens when he's embarrassed or angry, and Vander likes to make sure he's both. They've never gotten along.

At dusk, my friends begin to arrive. First the sisters, Salah and Lemon, giggling their thanks as Bessa offers them mugs of honeysuckle punch. Then Vander, with his usual sidekicks in tow, Basil and Petzyl, neither of whom was very kind to Rahz this afternoon. Jord, Cindra, and Nellie follow shortly thereafter. With the arrival of Bird, the gang's all here, all except one.

I peer out the window. The moon is huge, fully round and glowing purple, with a hazy halo all the way around. It's beautiful, but Rahz is nowhere in sight. My nerves itch under my skin.

Is he okay? Maybe he's more upset about today than I thought. He said he would be here. How long until I race to his house to check on him? What will the others think?

But I shouldn't have worried. He does come, late and last, and with a careful look on his face like he isn't sure how he'll be treated or if he's even welcome.

My heart jolts. I want to bring his smile back, but Bessa does it for me. Ever thoughtful, she's quick to put an apricot pastry in one of his hands and a mug of punch in the other.

Rahz's answering grin lights the room and sets a whole different kind of jitters stirring in my belly.

"There's a good lad. Go on, then. The others are downstairs already." She kisses his cheek and sends him toward me with a friendly swat to his rump.

I bump Rahz's shoulder with mine. "Thanks for coming."

He bumps me back. "Said I would," he mumbles around a mouthful of pastry.

We always gather in the low room, a carved-out space built into the earth under the rest of the cottage. As a result, it's cool, damp, and smells of wet rock, but best of all, my father usually ignores this room. It's my space and serves as our lair for round moon parties.

As soon as we shuffle down the stairs, Vander starts in on Rahz. "Get out the betting chips. We're going to play knuckle-bones. Think you can manage without cheating?"

Rahz balks on the bottom step, his gaze flitting to a giggling Salah and Lemon. But they aren't paying attention to Vander, and their laughter isn't at Rahz's expense, though he doesn't seem to know that. The girls are looking at each other, whispering secrets between themselves. Who knows what they thought was funny?

I missed an earlier chance to stand up for him, and I'm not about to let this one slip away. "Shut up. We all know *you're* the one who cheats at knucklebones."

Heads snap in our direction, the others eager to witness a squabble.

Vander scowls. "Do not."

Ignoring him, I grab Rahz's elbow and tug him to where the girls sit on floor cushions, sharing their snacks between them. Sometimes I wish I could get away with not inviting Vander, but Father says it's everyone or no one. That's what's fair.

We plop onto a worn cushion together. The velvet used to

be a vivid emerald green, but the fabric is faded and dusty now, the seams fraying around the gold corded edges.

Rahz folds himself up nearly as small as me. How does he do that with those long limbs of his? He's going to be a big man someday. Tall, broad, strong. Not like me. I'll be lucky to grow half his size. Jealousy curls in my belly, but it's not the mean kind. I'm glad for him. He'll be handsome. Sought after. Good for him.

As I get older, the desire to be *like* Rahz is getting confused with the desire to be *with* Rahz. To have him for myself. But we're just friends, and he doesn't think of me that way. I doubt he thinks of anyone that way. And if he does, he won't talk about it. I've nursed a little crush on him for as long as I can remember, but when I ask who he likes, he only blushes and refuses to say.

So I haven't told him.

Maybe I never will.

Vander's voice rises above the others. "We need new knuckle-bones. These are too old. They're worn on the flat side and don't roll properly anymore."

Petzyl shrugs. "They'll have to do."

"Or"—a crazed glint lights Vander's yellow eyes—"we could slaughter one of the neighbor's sheep. Get us a brand-new set."

My stomach drops. I know where knucklebones come from, but it's never occurred to me to kill a sheep to obtain a fresh set. As Vander's gaze settles on me, a gagging sensation tightens my throat.

I shake my head. "No. No way. We're not doing anything to bother the neighbors. I can't get into trouble again. My father might actually starve me this time."

"Slaughter a sheep for a stupid game?" Rahz sounds as disgusted as I feel. "There's something deeply wrong with you, Vander."

"Where else will we get new knucklebones, huh?"

"Nowhere," Salah says.

"We can play something else," Lemon adds.

"We have pick-up sticks." I gesture to the little cabinets built into the far wall containing our games and puzzles. "We haven't played that in a while."

"Because it's for children." Vander scoffs. "We're too old for that."

I roll my eyes, and to add another barrier between us and the neighbor's sheep, I kick off my sandals and shove them out of the way. The smooth river stones that make up the floor are cool against the sweaty soles of my feet. Rahz does the same. Then so do Salah and Lemon. Their solidarity makes me feel more relaxed. That and being next to Rahz. His presence always comforts me, like sliding into a familiar dance, one whose steps are long since memorized.

Rahz shifts on the cushion. "I have an idea."

"Who cares?" Vander's voice grates on my last nerve.

"Everyone but you, apparently," I say through gritted teeth.

We didn't use to fight so much. When we were younger, Vander's abrasive personality was easier to tolerate. None of us cared about who was fae, or who was human, or who was both. Those things only began to matter as the cycles passed, and our realm tightened around us with its politics, prejudices, and adult problems.

Vander is right about one thing. We aren't children anymore.

Sometimes I miss those simpler days. Other times, I wish to hurry and grow up. For the seasons to fly by so I can escape Father's strict rules and punishments. So I can manifest my magic. So I can finally meet my mother. So I can kiss a boy.

Maybe even Rahz.

"I have a new story," says Rahz, glowering at Vander. "And I bet I can scare you."

Vander casts him a skeptical glance. "Bet me what?"

"My knucklebones. I have a good set." Rahz leans into me

and lowers his voice. "Maybe that'll keep him away from the neighbor's sheep."

For now. We can hope.

Vander perks up. "Let me see."

"They're at home," says Rahz. "You'll have to trust me. What do I get if I win?"

"What do you want?"

Rahz taps his index finger to his chin and narrows his gaze. "For you to shut up whenever I say until the next round moon."

Vander sneers. "No way. I'm not letting you boss me around."

"Then you'd better not get scared."

"You can't scare me."

"Oh, I can."

The rest of the room has grown bored with their argument. Basil and Petzyl return to the snack tray Bessa left for us and fill their plates. The girls have their own conversation going and pay the bickering boys no mind.

I want to hear Rahz's new story, but he won't tell it right away. Best if we wait for the witching hour. When we're all tucked into our sleeping satchels and he has the best chance at scaring the wits out of Vander and the others. He's good at scaring me, but I don't mind. It's fun to be scared sometimes, especially when there's no real danger.

When Rahz is there to keep me safe.

Chapter Three

Rahz

We spread our sleeping satchels in a big circle around the room. At the center, Lemon casts an illumination spell, lighting our faces in a hazy golden glow. She's the first of us to begin to come into her magic, and we're all in awe of the dancing flame she conjured from seemingly nowhere.

I can't wait until my magic manifests. Sometimes I feel it inside me, growing big and strong, nearly ready to do my bidding. My hope is to become a powerful mage one day, so impressive that no one would dare bother me ever again.

But like all fae and mixling children, I must wait. Hopefully, not for too much longer, though.

Jindal is next to me, as usual, seated cross-legged on a pile of blankets and twiddling a half-eaten sugar stick between his fingers.

The air in the low room is chilly and damp, but I'm warm in my flannel satchel. All eyes are on me, and for once, I don't mind. Telling stories is what I'm good at, thanks to my mother's little library. I want the others to watch. To lean forward, eager for the next detail. To cower at the scary bits. I want all of it.

With a deep breath, I begin, "Once upon a time—"

Vander scoffs loudly. "You think a kiddie tale that starts with 'Once upon a time' is going to scare me?"

I scowl. "Yes."

"Now shut your mouth so we can hear it." Jindal's earnest defense sparks a warm flutter in me. I'd already forgiven him for not siding with me at lessons, but now I'm feeling sheepish at having doubted him in the first place. He's obviously on my side.

"Let's try this again." I lower my voice. "Once upon a time, many cycles ago, when the gate between the worlds still stood wide open and our realm was young, a terrible creature crossed through from the other side. A creature with glowing red eyes, a snarling mouth, and teeth as sharp as daggers. He was starving and near to mindless from hunger. But not just any food would do." I pause for effect. "The creature needed blood. Lots of it."

Salah and Lemon scoot closer together. Vander isn't fazed, but this is only the beginning. I'm not worried. I'll get him.

"The only way to slake his desperate thirst was to kill his victims and drink them dry." I lick my lips. "He'd already slaughtered so many people in his realm that those who remained had armed themselves. Fought together. Stalked him and forced him to retreat north.

"Night by night, he'd made his way through the snow and ice to the grand gate and our magical realm, where he'd be free to attack our innocent, our vulnerable, our young, and our old. He'd slay them to satiate his endless appetite for blood. That was his plan. But he didn't know what was waiting. *Who* was waiting. For the Gatekeeper stood at the ready, his only job to protect Luminia from threat."

"Seriously?" Vander again, his bushy brows climbing his forehead. "The Gatekeeper is the hero of this story? We're supposed to believe that freak is the good guy?"

"Shh." Salah and Lemon shush him together.

"You'll have to keep listening to find out. If you keep interrupting me, I'll stop the story, and we'll all go to bed."

To my delight, a chorus of protest sweeps the room.

Vander sneers. "Then you forfeit, and I win."

Even Basil and Petzyl are annoyed with him. "Just let him finish," says Basil.

"Yeah, you don't know what's going to happen yet," says Petzyl.

Vander grunts, "Fine," and folds his arms over his chest.

I shake my head. "The Gatekeeper had never come face-to-face with such a beastly foe, never encountered such other-worldly strength, though he'd heard whispers of the likes of a creature such as this one. A vampire.

"Most of the beings on the other side of the gate are weaker than us, human and short-lived, not a threat to the mighty fae. But on this fateful night, the Gatekeeper would learn of vampires firsthand. A monster capable of drinking blood by the barrel full. A monster whose thirst could never be slaked. A monster whose mind was lost to its demons. Worse even than incubi and nigh impossible to kill."

We've known about vampires on our side of the gate for centuries, but they're few and far between. None of us has ever seen one. They've been tamed since the old legends and integrated into society, but no amount of good manners can make up for the source of their dark power.

Our blood.

A shiver vibrates through me. I'm not the only one affected. Poor Jindal is curled into a tight ball tangled in blankets. His eyes are wide and so, so orange. Like ripened pumpkins and nearly as big. And I haven't gotten to the worst part yet.

"The Gatekeeper fought valiantly with sword and fists, but no blow could keep the vampire down. No slash could stop the relentless attack of the undead. The creature could not be hobbled. It wouldn't stop lunging for the Gatekeeper's throat.

"As the battle raged on, the Gatekeeper grew tired. The scent of blood spiced the air like molten iron from the forge. He weakened and cried out for help, but none would come to his aid, for his castle was filled with slaves. And what slave would risk their own life for that of their master?"

A knock from the top of the stairs startles us from the tale. Vander nearly jumps out of his satchel, and I chuckle. It's only Bessa coming to check on us.

"I'm for bed." She's unaware we're all coiled like springs. "You lot need anything before I go?"

"No, Bessa, thanks," I call out. "We're good."

"Thanks, Bessa," the others chime.

"Night, night, then. Sweet dreams." Her footsteps creep away, and we're alone again.

"Now, where were we?" I ask.

"The Gatekeeper is losing his fight against the vampire," says Salah.

"What happens next?" asks Lemon.

I sit up straighter to finish the tale. "With great sorrow, the Gatekeeper realized all hope was lost. His defeat was inevitable. The gate would be unprotected for the first time in millennia. The monster would be free to continue his onslaught of the innocent people of his palace. And our realm would be in mortal peril." The last two words I emphasize with a dire tone.

No matter how unsavory the Gatekeeper might be, we all know we owe our lives to his protection. Even if he's just as scary as whatever lies on the other side of the great northern gate. He stands guard so the rest of us can live in peace.

I paint the picture with my words. "Blood coated his hands, ran in crimson rivulets down his neck, and slicked the stone ground beneath his feet as he struggled. He'd go down fighting, but it wouldn't be enough. The creature's snarling growls echoed loudly in his ears. He couldn't let that be the last sound he'd ever hear.

"A spark of an idea formed, dim at first, then flaming with intensity. 'Turn me!' the Gatekeeper howled. 'Turn me into a vampire like you!'

"'Why should I when I could kill you instead?' demanded the vampire. The Gatekeeper's blood stained his lips a gruesome red.

"'You will need a guide in this realm. Who better than me? You've seen my strength. My will to live. Turn me, and I'll be your willing slave. Think of the power you'll wield, with me in your thrall.'

"The vampire narrowed his eyes, considering the plea. The offer. He studied the Gatekeeper, gaze roaming from head to toe to the tip of each mighty black wing. He gave a slow nod. 'Yes, yes, you might prove useful to me. I will do it.' He beckoned with the crook of his skeletal finger. 'Come here.'

"The Gatekeeper's gut sank. Though it was his own idea, and though it was the only way out, he didn't want to give up his life to the fiend. What would happen? When humans were turned, they became vampires, undead, unable to walk in the sunlight or feel the beating of their hearts ever again. But the Gatekeeper was full fae. Would it be different for him? Was it worth what he would lose?

"None of that mattered. He had no other choice but to die a true death and leave his beloved realm unprotected. He had to try this, no matter the cost.

"On shaky legs, the Gatekeeper crept forward. The vampire lunged, growling his delight with a cackling laugh that sent shivers down the Gatekeeper's spine.

"Trapped in the arms of the fiend with nothing to do but surrender, the Gatekeeper focused on the strong *thump thump thump* of his heart. If this was to be the last time he'd feel it, he wished to remember.

"Fangs pierced his throat, fast and deep. He cried out as the vampire closed his jaws over the vulnerable flesh. He told himself he wasn't really giving in. He was stealing the creature's strength, stealing the curse for himself, and becoming powerful enough to fight back and win.

"His eyes shuttered closed at the thought. *I will win. I must.*"

I pause, glancing around the room at the others. They're leaning in. Salah and Lemon clutch each other's hands. Jindal has bitten his lower lip raw. But best of all, Vander is hugging his arms around himself, just as enthralled as the rest. I'm definitely winning our little bet. I raise my brows at him to let him know it. He scowls but makes no protest.

"As the vampire swallowed his life's blood down his gullet one greedy gulp at a time, the Gatekeeper grew weak in his arms. The rotten, sickly scent of death became stronger, and he feared he would be next. He'd made a terrible mistake. But just when he thought the worst would come to pass, the vampire stopped. Drew back. And with a wicked, glinting grin, brought his wrist to his mouth and bit.

"The wound bled freely. The Gatekeeper's gaze was drawn to it like a moth to a flame. His stomach rumbled, and an incredible thirst rose like lava from an erupting volcano. A compulsion unlike any other gripped him. He must drink. He needed that blood. Would do anything to get it.

"Though the very idea revolted him, the Gatekeeper parted his lips as the vampire pressed the wound to his mouth. Fighting back nausea, he resigned himself to his fate. A blood drinker. Cursed. But the first taste shocked him with its delicious decadence. Hot, savory, and spiced like copper cookware, it burned a path down his throat to his core. He lit up from the inside. 'More! Give me more!'

"The vampire let him drink his fill, and the Gatekeeper was greedy in his thirst. His heart never stopped beating. It only grew louder and louder. The racing *thump thump thump* pounded like a mallet on a drum, faster and faster as he consumed the most forbidden of nectars.

"The vampire ripped the bloody wound away from him, and the Gatekeeper yowled at the loss. 'Enough,' said the vampire, but the Gatekeeper yearned for more. Already his strength was returning. Doubling. Tripling. His muscles tensed and fluttered beneath his skin, eager to finish the fight. Fangs burst through his gums, new and deadly sharp, cutting his lower lip in two places.

"His ragged breaths huffed cool air through his lungs, not icy like his home but not warm like other living beings either. He shuddered. What had he done?"

Salah chimed in, "Did it work?"

"Did the Gatekeeper defeat the vampire?" asked Lemon.

I glare at them for interrupting. Not meanly. I like that they're so caught up in my tale they speak out of turn. They quiet down.

Jindal scoots closer to me and whispers, "What happened next, Rahz?"

A smile curls my lips. "The Gatekeeper straightened to his full height, and the vampire realized at once what he'd done. The fatal mistake he'd made. One that might mean his true death.

"They squared up again, circling as each attempted to stare the other down. 'You're no match for me, fledgling,' said the vampire, but what did he know? He'd never encountered a fae before, and the Gatekeeper's bloodline is the most powerful of our entire realm.

"The fight was brutal, tooth and nail, wing and claw, but the Gatekeeper had an edge now. He'd win this fight, and win he did, standing over the vampire in victory, both of them raw and bloodied. 'You should not have invaded Luminia. But don't let it be said I show no mercy. For your crimes, you may choose your fate. Either I take your head, thus granting you a true death, or you may live out your immortal years imprisoned in my dungeons. Choose.'"

"What did the vampire pick?" Jindal's voice is soft, hesitant. He clutches the edge of his sleep satchel, wringing it between his hands.

"What do you think?" I ask. "Did the Gatekeeper saw off his head and leave him in pieces? Or does the demon rot in the dark, dank dungeon to this very night?"

"I think he's in the dungeon," says Salah. Lemon nods her agreement.

"No," says Petzyl. "He wouldn't choose to suffer for all eternity. Better off dead."

"Head cut off for sure." Basil backs him up.

I shrug. "No one knows. And no one ever will. The Gatekeeper is a master at keeping secrets and allows no visitors to his frozen palace."

My audience is silent, each of them processing the tale in their own way. Vander's jaw is clenched, lips pressed to a tight line. He knows he's lost—I definitely scared him—but will he admit it? I have my doubts.

"That's a stupid ending," he says. "You didn't even tell us what happened."

I roll my eyes. "Sometimes stories end that way, whether you like it or not. Sometimes the ending is for you to determine."

He scowls. "Well, you didn't scare me."

"Yes, I did. I saw you over there shivering in your sleep sack. Don't pretend you weren't."

"Was not."

"Was so," say Salah and Lemon together.

As much as I like having the others come to my defense, I don't care if I won or not. So long as Vander leaves me alone. "Lie all you want. I'm tired. I'm going to sleep, and it won't be *me* having nightmares."

Chapter Four

Jindal

Panic surges through me. My chest is tight, and my heart is beating so fast I'm afraid it will seize any second. Can a person live in this much terror? Can I?

The Gatekeeper's long black hair tickles my cheeks as he looms over me, ice-blue eyes piercing deep into my soul. "Come, little one. With me forevermore." His voice is gentle, mesmerizing but no less frightening for its softness.

I shake my head frantically and grip my blankets in clenched fists. "No, you can't have me. I won't go."

He leans in closer. His winter-cold breath chills me to the bone. Sharp teeth gleam pearlescent from an even sharper smile. "But you're all alone. Younglings with dormant parents can't survive on their own. You need me."

"I don't." I have parents, don't I? My mom is sleeping, but Father counts. He has to. "My father—"

"Is as good as dormant, sweetling. You cannot lie to the prince of lies."

Long fingers with sleek black talons reach for me. Ebony wings shade all light from view. I toss and turn, fighting to escape his clutches, but it's too late. The Gatekeeper's got me.

I scream.

H ANDS SQUEEZE MY SHOULDERS. I STRUGGLE, BUT MY fight is doomed to failure. Should I accept my fate gracefully? No parents, so I belong to the Gatekeeper now. Rules are rules. Maybe I should give in.

"Jindal." My name whispered in my ear. Warm breath. Not cold. "Jindal, wake up." A familiar voice. Not the cloying croon of the Gatekeeper.

Rahz.

A warm flutter stirs in my belly. He firms his grip and gives me a gentle shake.

I open my eyes to find him very close, green eyes blazing with concern.

"Jinny, wake up."

"Rahz?"

A relieved sigh dampens my cheek. "Thank the Gatherdawn. You're awake."

I blink, and the more I blink, the more the horrid dream fades away. My breath comes in shuddering gasps. My heart thuds against my ribs. But I'm awake, the Gatekeeper is gone, and Rahz is here. "It wasn't real."

"You were having a nightmare." Rahz cups my face in his sweaty palms. "You're safe with me."

His words splash over me like fresh water from the hot springs, washing away the remnants of fear. Safe. With Rahz. Yes.

But just when I calm down, a new worry rises to the fore. We aren't alone. I glance around the room in dismay. Did I wake the others? Do they know?

A low snore comes from the lump that is Vander all curled up in his bedding. Asleep. Phew. The room is still and quiet. My shame is my own.

Well, Rahz knows too. But that's all right. Rahz won't make fun of me for it. He is too good to make someone else feel bad.

"You feeling better?" he whispers.

Still shaky, but I nod. "It seemed so real."

"Nightmares always do."

"You have them too?" It's hard to imagine big, strong Rahz succumbing to night terrors like me.

"Sometimes." He drops his hands to his lap. I miss their warmth. Their comfort. "Want to talk about it?"

Another snore from Vander. I scrunch my nose. "Not here."

"The garden?"

"Yes." We shuffle out of our flannel nests and sneak upstairs together, careful on the fourth step, which we both know creaks as loud as a rooster's crow. Our bare feet are silent on the floorboards as we creep through the cottage to the back door.

Outside, the round moon shines silvery purple on the flagstones. We sit under the vine-covered pergola on a little stone bench, side by side. Close enough for our thighs to touch. His presence is soothing.

"What happened?"

I tell him. It's not the first time I've had this dream, and I'm sure it won't be the last. But this time felt so real. "I could smell his breath, Rahz. Like spearmint and pine, colder than ice, rippling across my cheek with every word. As if he was really here, waiting to take me with him to his ice castle."

"That must have been scary." He takes my hand. His palm is hot. Nothing like the frigid touch of the Gatekeeper. "I'm so sorry. This is my fault."

"No, it isn't."

"I shouldn't have told that story. It triggered your dream."

"Maybe. Maybe not. Anyway, it's not your fault. I know the

legends. What the Gatekeeper does. Who he steals. I've always been afraid one day he'll come for me."

"He won't. The stories aren't real."

"They might be."

"Even if they are, you have your father."

Do I? But I can't put voice to that thought. Too dangerous. Saying it out loud makes it more real, and that's the last thing I want. "What are your nightmares about?"

Rahz turns away and casts his gaze downward.

Regret slams me sideways. I didn't mean to make him uncomfortable, especially when he's kind enough to comfort me. "You don't have to say if you don't want to."

"No, it's all right. You're my best friend. I can tell you." Rahz takes a deep breath. A shadow crosses his face, and his gaze takes on a faraway quality. He looks older like this, and I see a hint of the man he will become someday. I like what I see.

"I dream of war," he says. "Of fighting. I dream we need soldiers, and I am called to serve. So I go to battle, even though it frightens me. I don't want to fight. I only wish for peace, but sometimes peace must be fought for. There's blood and pain and death. And like your dream, it all seems real. The screams, the metallic scent in the air, the groans of the dying." He trembles. "If I close my eyes, I can hear them, even now."

I squeeze his hand. "I wonder why you dream such things when Luminia has been at peace for ages."

His gaze falls on me like a rainstorm. "And what guarantee have we that it will stay that way?"

"Why would things change?"

"Because things always do."

I think on that. Perhaps it's true for Rahz, but not for me. My life changes little from day to day. Attend my lessons, mind my father, stay out of his way, and help Bessa with the chores. Same old, same old.

But Rahz lives with his mother. His human mother. A fact I haven't given a whole lot of thought before this. He has only a mother, and I have only a father. Between us, we have the whole set. But what must it be like to be human among so many fae? And to be a hybrid of the two, like Rahz?

A sad reality dawns on me. Rahz will lose his mother someday. Her kind doesn't live as long as ours. Whereas I might someday go dormant like my mother, Rahz's mom will actually die. And he's never known his father, whose heritage will grant Rahz a long life like mine.

Rahz is destined to be alone.

Tears blur my vision as I grip his hand even tighter, bringing it to my chest and holding his palm over my heart.

"What is it?" he asks, turning to face me.

I sniffle and shake my head. He's known for his whole life what I've only just realized. He doesn't need to hear me say it. "Nothing."

"It's definitely not nothing," he huffs. He lets go of my hand and wipes the tears from my cheeks with his thumbs. Then he slings an arm around me, drawing me in. "Don't be afraid. We're safe here together."

Warmth floods my chest. I stare at his mouth. We're so close. If I leaned in, just a little, I could—

Rahz kisses me, bridging the gap between us and pressing our lips together gently. A quick peck. There and gone. In that second, my entire world rearranges itself.

My body alights with a tingling rush of sensation that curls my toes and flutters my wings. I lick my lips to taste him there and nearly moan at the sensation.

His cheeks are pink, and he's turning away.

No, no, no.

I grab his face and bring it back to mine. This time, when we kiss, the touch lingers. Soft and warm. Our mouths pressed together, parting slightly to fit even closer. I breathe through my nose so I don't have to pull away. Tasting sweet apricots and sugar, I'm swooning, floating, even though my wings lay folded on my back.

I don't know what to do—this is my first kiss, er, well, second if I count that little peck he just gave me—I only know I never want this moment to end.

Rahz's hands are hot on my waist. Mine cup his nape under the silky-soft weight of his silver hair. I chase him as he pulls away, and both of us grin.

"Feel better?" he asks shyly, his cheeks still pink as lollyberries.

Whatever upset me is a distant memory that pales compared to his lovely, shining lips. "Mm-hmm." I dart in to kiss him again, but he stops me with a hand braced on my sternum.

"Jindal, slow down."

I search his face and find no answer. "Why?"

Rahz stands. He's so much bigger than me. I want to climb him and cling like a sloth, press my nose into his hair, and breathe him in. My best friend. My crush. My Rahz.

But the vulnerable look to his expression concerns me. Maybe he doesn't feel the same way I feel after all. My heart sinks. Was that kiss only to make me feel better? Is there no deeper meaning?

I wring my hands in my lap, stewing over my next words carefully. "Sorry I tried to maul you."

A slow smile lifts his lips and shoos away my undue worry. "It's not that. I *liked* that." He hides his flushed face behind his hand, rubbing his thumb and forefinger over his brows. "I've wanted to kiss you for a long time. This means something to me. I need to know it means something to you too before we"—he drops his hand and flutters his fingers between us in a frantic little motion I find perfectly adorable—"before we—"

I'm on my feet and hugging him to my chest so he doesn't have to fret a second longer.

"Oof, okay." He hugs me back.

I bury my face in his neck and mumble, "It means *everything* to me."

"You mean *everything* to me too."

Next, we learn *a lot* about kissing together.

Chapter Five

~Ten Years Later~

Rahz

Kissing Jindal is my favorite hobby. It's better than racing my favorite horse, Magna, better than binging on Bessa's delectable pastries, even better than practicing my unruly magic. Nothing beats the soft, needy whimpers he makes as I ravish his mouth with mine.

I walk him backward through the barn to the wooden ladder that leads to our loft, my hands on his hips. We stall here for some time, him standing on the first rung, me caging him with my body. Like this, we're the same height, perfect for indulging in our favorite pastime.

Kissing...and all that follows.

Our work today is finished. The animals have been cared for, the neighbor's old fence mended, and the supper dishes washed and put away. Jindal's father has the cottage to himself for the night, and we have our loft.

"Take me to bed, Rahz," Jindal murmurs against my lips.

I chuckle. "I'm trying. Up the stairs you get."

After a sweet kiss, he turns and climbs the ladder. I swat his bottom to hurry him along, then scurry up after him.

At the top is a wide ledge, big enough for the feather mattress we stuffed ourselves, two sets of drawers, and a little table with lounge pillows for seats. We don't live here, not really, but we sleep here more often than not. I still have my room in my mother's house, and Jindal has his place in his father's cottage. But we've claimed the barn loft as our own, and it's cozier than either of our proper houses.

In his rush to undress, Jindal flings his clothes everywhere. Blood rushes south as I admire each bit of peachy-pink skin he reveals—the lithe line of his spine curving while he tugs off his shirt, the muscles of his shoulders bunching, the perky mounds of his bottom bouncing as he shimmies out of his breeches.

He catches me watching, and a wide grin splits his face. "Like what you see?"

"You know I do." I palm my cock, which is steadfastly growing too big for my leather pants. Jindal has this effect on me often. I have to be careful what I think about as we work side by side through the day so as not to embarrass myself with desire for him. He's a hard worker despite his tendency to tease and play. His muscles must be sore from digging all the postholes for the fence repair. When he's satiated and boneless, I'll give him a massage. Work the knots out. But not yet. After.

I lick my lips, mouth watering at the sight of his pretty cock jutting proudly from a patch of silky purple curls. He flops onto his back on our nest of blankets, legs parted, one straight and the other drawn up, as if he knows how irresistible that pose is to me. With a single crooked finger, he beckons.

Hurriedly, I add my clothes to the haphazard pile and join

him. Jindal opens his arms for me, and I slot myself between his legs and drop my weight onto his chest. Our kisses are heated, wet, and sloppy as our bodies find a rhythm together, grinding and pressing in the practiced way we've developed over the years.

By the round moon, I love this. Love him. Love the life we're building together, one project at a time. If only everything could stay this way, just like this, for centuries, but my fear urges me to treasure our peace while it lasts. The future is uncertain. Our world is changing.

Jindal draws me from my thoughts by sneaking a hand between us and wrapping it around our cocks. I ignore the world beyond our loft and fuck into his fist. Slow, lazy strokes turn urgent as our pleasure builds.

I tangle my fingers in his hair, grab a fistful, and tug just the way he likes. A delightful moan escapes his lips. He tips his head, offering his neck. I suck a mark into his skin that he'll complain about in the morning but only teasingly. Not-so-secretly, I know he likes wearing my marks, or I wouldn't make them.

"Want you now." He arches and squirms, drawing up his knees.

"Yes." I nibble his throat over the mark and shift downward to align our bodies. A bit of magic slicks the way for us, a path we know well.

We fit together like two halves of the same soul, his body opening for mine, mine filling his, even as he cries out for more. We've perfected this dance. We know how to draw out each sensation. How to build the enticing pressure between us to its zenith. How to revel in our shared ecstasy, shuddering on the edge for as long as our bodies allow.

As our rhythm reaches a crescendo and sweat dampens our heated skin, the pleasured gasps and groans Jindal shudders out increase in frequency. My favorite part, and not only for the obvious reasons of our shared release but because his sweet noises make my heart race and my toes curl. I love hearing his bliss, knowing I'm part of it, that we can do this for each other.

Here with Jindal, coming apart in his arms as he vibrates, his cock spurting between us, I know peace. Nothing can touch me here but him. Not the list of chores to be done, not the stress of worry over our future, not the whispers of uprisings in the south. Only Jindal. My lover. My partner.

I'm gasping, buzzing, my heart is racing, and my body is pulsing as I come inside him. It feels so good I have to close my eyes against one sensation too many. Jindal squeezes his thighs around my torso, digs his heels in my ass, and rakes his fingernails down my back, leaving a tingling line of pleasure-pain in their wake. Love that. I bury my face in his neck and inhale. Mmm. That scent. His delicious sweet, woody smell, like cedar and lilac. I can't get enough.

Slowly, as fevered euphoria melts into warm fading pleasure, we relax. Jindal presses more kisses against my hair. He trails soft fingertips over the nail marks he's made. They're probably already fading. He didn't scratch me that hard.

I ease our bodies apart and call up my magic, bidding it to clear the mess from our skin.

Jindal smiles up at me and swipes my hair behind my ear. The silent conversation between us goes like this.

Good?

So good. You?

Yes. Love you.

Love you too.

We don't always need words to say what we're feeling anymore, not after ten years of companionship, love, and trust.

I kneel between his legs. "Roll over."

His gaze carries a question, but he doesn't ask it, just does what I say. He shuffles onto his belly, and I straddle him, using his delectable bottom as a seat. Carefully, I push his wings out of my way. He gets the hint and unfolds them, revealing the shimmering pink skin of his back.

I get to work, kneading the tight muscles under my fingers.

He groans. "Oh, Rahz, yes."

I chuckle. I'm not sure he sounded quite that pleased when I was fucking him. "Sore?"

"I guess I am. I hadn't realized."

"You worked hard today."

"So did you."

I didn't, though, not as hard as Jindal. I relied mostly on my magic, whereas he had only a shovel and the strength of his body.

He has magic too, but not like mine. Jindal can cast simple spells, move light objects, call a fair bit of water, and urge seedlings to sprout. Normal things. But me? My magic moves mountains. It can invade minds, though I try not to, and render me all but invisible if I don't want to be seen. I'm not certain why it's so strong, with only half my heritage being fae, but it's sure made my life easier. There are legends of other mixlings such as me, with magic such as mine, but I've never met any of them.

What I do know is that no one picks on me anymore. That boon would be enough by itself, but in addition, anytime someone in the village needs any real work done, I'm the one they call. And of course where I go, Jindal goes. So today, I felled trees, cut and modified branches to the right size, moved them into place, and set them in the series of holes Jindal dug as I worked. Together we patched the entire fence in the span of one afternoon. We make such a good team.

He moans again as I work the knots out, moving down the length of his spine with my thumbs. I admire his wings, no longer jealous like I was when we were young, just happy to bear witness to the joy flying brings him. He's quick and agile in the air, like a butterfly but even prettier. Sometimes I take Magna out for a ride through the country while Jindal races along above us, light as air and fast as a windstorm.

I put my weight into the massage, dragging my hands over his shoulders, down his arms, and back to his neck until every tight muscle has turned to putty beneath my fingers. Then I gather his delicate wings, tuck them in the way he likes, and lie down next to him.

He rolls to face me, his expression dopey as though he's high off poppy. He's so cute like this. "Thanks, Rahz." Even his voice has a dreamy quality to it.

"My pleasure." Our knees bump as we curl into each other.

He gives a half-hearted push on my shoulder. "Roll over. I'll do you."

"I'm good." Besides, I just want to look at him. I'll never tire of his lovely face. Those orange eyes stare straight into my soul.

"You sure? Because that was amazing, and you look like you need it too."

"Another time." My stress isn't of the bodily variety but of the mind. A simple massage won't help. "Plus, you look about as strong as a wet noodle right now."

He presses a fingertip to my nose and smooshes. "Your fault."

"Indeed." I nibble his fingertip.

His gaze narrows. "What's wrong?"

A sigh escapes unbidden. It's impossible to hide anything from Jindal. He reads me like a book. "We don't need to talk about it now. You're tired."

"Not too tired for you. Tell me. What's got this crinkle in your forehead making an appearance?" He runs his finger over it as if to soothe, and I try to relax my face.

Best be out with it, then. "Vander says there's fighting in the south between the humans and the fae. Whispers of a human uprising."

Jindal frowns. "Since when do you listen to what Vander has to say?"

"Since he returned from the merchant routes through Lemossin. I don't think he'd lie about this, Jin. It's too important."

"I don't trust Vander. Probably he wanted to rile you up."

I shake my head. "I think he was trying to get a handle on where I'd stand if I had to choose. Fae or human? And it's not just Vander. He isn't the only one worried about this."

Jindal scrunches his brow and stiffens. "My father doesn't count."

"Why not?"

"He gets his rumors from the gossips in Clodhill. You know how they can be. Always poking around in everyone's business."

"Just because they're unsavory doesn't mean they're wrong."

The quality of Jindal's gaze shifts, like he's peering into my soul and finds a bit of dust to be swept away. "You're really worried about this?"

"You're not?"

"We're quite far away from Lemossin and even farther from the southern shores of Irondale. It's safe here in Jodpirn."

"For now."

He blinks. "Luminia has been peaceful for millennia. Not since the war with incubi have we squabbled. Our society works. The four fae bloodlines rule, and we all prosper. Why would anyone want to fight?"

I bite my tongue. Do we all prosper? I'm not so sure. What of Bessa? We love her, yes, and she loves us, but what would her life have been if she'd been free to choose her fate? If she hadn't needed work? If Jindal's father hadn't hired her to care for his baby when Jindal's mother went dormant? Would she have a family of her own? Children? These are the sorts of things I've been wondering about and haven't got any answers for.

And there's my own mother to consider. A human who

raised her mixed-blood child all alone when my fae father couldn't be bothered. We're treated well enough, but the other mothers weren't expected to clean the schoolhouse on weekends. Weren't expected to scrub floors, polish silver, or wax windows. No, those chores always fell to the humans among us, and everyone acted as if this were fair and normal, but I can't help but wonder why.

Why aren't we all equal?

No, not everyone prospers in Luminia. At least not the same amount.

Jindal kisses me, a gentle press of lips, followed by a whisper. "You've left me out of the conversation again. What are you thinking about so hard that you can't say it aloud?"

I didn't mean for this to happen. We've had such a nice day and an even better night. I want to snuggle him close and drift off to a dreamless sleep with the smell of his hair in my nose.

Maybe there's nothing to worry about after all. Maybe he's right. The south is so far away, and things here are peaceful.

"I'm sorry I brought it up."

He purses his lips at my nonanswer but doesn't push. Sweet Jindal. Neither of us likes to argue, but sometimes that means simple disagreements fester. This doesn't feel simple, and I'm not ready to pick through the thorns this conversation would bring up. Another day. Another night.

"You can always talk to me." He tucks his head beneath my chin.

I tighten my arms around him and pull us as close as two people can be. "I know."

But I don't.

Chapter Six

THE BREEZE IN MY HAIR IS LIGHT AND COOL, EVEN AS my heart is heavy as stone. Seated astride sweet Magna—Rahz's favorite horse, who he insisted I borrow for the afternoon—I'm closing in on my destination.

Usually, I'd fly, but my back muscles are sore, and Rahz thought a nice ride would be easier on me. Besides, it's always lovely to have Magna for company.

I don't make this trip often. There's not much I like about Clodhill. The neighboring village is bigger than Jodpirn and, as such, has more choices in shops, foods, and activities. But along with size come all the problems associated with a large population: more petty crime, more waste, and more disagreements over resources.

Plus, Father likes Clodhill, so my contrary nature demands my distaste. But I do come here at least once a year on this day, Mother's birthday, to say hello and pay my respects.

I can't see her—viewings are forbidden by the guardians—

but I can be near her where she rests in the Temple of Light. Can she sense my presence? Am I a comfort to her as she sleeps? I don't know the answers, but I can't help dwelling on the questions as Magna walks us into town.

Some fae, when they wake from dormancy, have memories from their time at rest, and some don't. One thing I know for sure. If my mother wakes up with memories, my visits will be among them. I want her to know how important she is to me, even though we've yet to meet. She will know my devotion never waned as she rested, unlike Father's.

Magna ambles straight to the stables without any prompting from me. She makes this trip more often than I do. Rahz actually likes Clodhill, and as such, he and Magna take care of any town business for both of us.

But he can't do this for me.

I leave Magna in the care of a friendly stable hand, a human girl of maybe sixteen or seventeen cycles with long brown hair tied back at her nape. She greets the horse in a familiar fashion and offers a handful of sweet-smelling honeypods, which Magna gobbles down with the gusto of an animal starved, though I can attest she ate a heaping helping of breakfast only a few hours prior.

"Thank you." I nod to the girl. "Don't spoil her too much, or she won't want to leave with me later."

She grins. "Have no fear, good sir. Rahz has this lady wrapped around his little finger. No doubt she'll be eager to return to him."

I stroke Magna's long neck. "You're absolutely correct."

The stable hand clicks her tongue, and the two of them saunter off together.

I stuff my hands into my pockets and set off on the longer route through the edges of town to avoid the bustle of the main roads. More time to think this way, and my mind wanders first and always to Rahz. His schedule is full these days, with everyone vying for the use of his magic for whatever project they're too lazy to do themselves.

His sorcery is both a blessing and a curse. Wonderful to have such power at his disposal and to have grown up a respected member of the community, one valued for his many contributions. Yet there's no denying the burden rests heavily on his shoulders.

His big, broad, muscular shoulders.

I giggle. Those are all mine. Others may look, but only I can touch.

Rahz doesn't seem to mind the villagers' reliance on him. He likes to work. To help. To till the earth, mend the fences, harvest the vegetables, shingle the roofs, and whatever else they ask of him. "It's easier for me," he says, his tone casual. "With my magic, I can accomplish in two hours what would take four men an entire day." He shrugs this off as unimportant. "Why shouldn't I help?"

And it's not like I don't think he should help, only that I wish he had more time for his own pursuits. Riding Magna, quiet mornings with his mother, evenings reading books, telling stories, and not to be forgotten, fucking me senseless.

But we make sure to find plenty of time for that.

I pass a row of squat cottages, smaller than the one I share with Father and a fair bit shabbier too. These are human neighborhoods on the outskirts of the city where many of the town's workers live. Little garden plots make up the front yards. Tumbling vines laden with the colorful squash of the late season twist and meander toward the road. The air smells of dusky incense, burned to cover the scent of the wastewater as it drains from the center of town to the wildlands beyond.

Another reason I prefer Jodpirn. In our village, used water is rerouted directly to our fields to be gobbled up by hungry plants. No time to get smelly. No need for heavy incense. But

Jodpirn doesn't have a temple where dormant fae can rest safely, and Clodhill does. So here I am.

My leather shoes are silent on the brown cobbles as I near the city center. Around me, the noise of the hustle and bustle of town rises to a crescendo. Fae folk going about their business, street vendors hawking their wares, the ringing chime of a bell as someone zooms past on a wheeled swift walker.

I let the flurry of activity wash over me in an effort to remain unbothered. But where I'm going, all will be still. All will be silent. In only a few more blocks, my destination will be at hand, and I can escape the din of the streets.

"Flowers, sir?" A young human boy with huge brown eyes thrusts a bouquet at my chest. I have to shuffle sideways so as not to barrel right into him. "Handpicked from the warm southern lands," he says. "Beautiful, like you. Exotic. Only the best, most fragrant varieties. On sale too."

I shake my head and make to press on, but he persists, tagging along beside me.

"Just one, sir? Orange, like your eyes. To wear behind your ear, perhaps?"

Pausing, I look him over. His face is clean, but his clothes are dirty. His feet are bare, even as the chill of the season has crept in. Though he's a child, perhaps twelve or thirteen, he's nearly as tall as me already, but skinny. Very skinny.

If selling imported flowers on the street is what he does for work, he couldn't make much, but that's no reason for him to appear so underfed. Clodhill is a thriving city with more than enough resources to feed its people. Why has this boy gone hungry?

He holds the bouquet too close to my face. I squint and step back. He's correct; they're beautiful flowers, the likes of which I've never laid eyes on, but then, I've never traveled to the southern regions. I've never traveled past Clodhill. I like Jodpirn. Rahz is there, so I have no reason to leave.

With a sigh, I decide to part with some of my coin for this boy. "How much?"

"For the orange flower or the bouquet?" His grin is so hopeful it strikes a bitter taste in my mouth.

"Both."

He names his price. Too much, but I don't haggle. I hand over the coin, and he presents the bouquet, but the single orange flower he bravely tucks behind my ear, moving my hair and skimming the sensitive skin beneath the lobe with rough fingers quite purposefully.

He leans in and says quietly, almost shyly, as though this part is new to him, "Would you like *company*, perhaps? I know a place."

As my mind reluctantly parses out his meaning, I reel backward. Is a youngster in the street propositioning a full-grown man? How has Clodhill sunk to this? Does Rahz know? Does my father?

Would he even care?

"No, thank you," I stutter the words out and hurry away from him. My mother is waiting. I can't think of this now. The temple is just ahead. In my rush to leave the crowds on the main path, I break into a trot.

By the time I'm climbing the great marble staircase to the temple's entrance, I'm out of breath, and my heart is racing. My mind can't wrap itself around the boy's situation, so instead, it offers me excuses. Perhaps he just liked the look of me. He's of an age when those particular desires begin to manifest. He's an early bloomer, looking to gain a new experience, that's all. Nothing sordid going on. Nothing amuck in Clodhill. All is well. He's probably already busy eating a steaming bowl of meat and vegetable stew with the coin he's made on his overpriced flowers.

He's fine.

Telling myself such lies and believing them are two different things, and only one is working for me. But I must shove the thoughts aside. The temple is a pure place, not meant for inelegant musings, and the divine elders must have no reason to bar my entry.

I bow to a robed guardian and walk through to the inner courtyard, then take a seat on a stone bench and unlace my shoes. I set them aside and slip on the soft temple sandals provided to visitors who pass beyond this point. I'm used to this ritual.

The strong scent of warmed cedar oil tickles my nostrils. I scrunch my nose to hold in a sneeze. Mother's resting place is down a set of steps and through an arched doorway that leads to a large cavern with rows and rows of matching dormancy cradles. The soft beds are suspended from the ceiling like hammocks, fully contained nests of colorful silken sheets, feathered pillows, and decorated corded tassels as if trying to make what's essentially an extended coma look cheerful. Each has a plaque labeled with the name of the sleeping fae inside, along with the date they fell asleep. In my mother's case, that date is also my birthday, which is why I think it's fitting for me to visit on hers.

My chest tightens. It always does when I'm here. There's something oddly uncomfortable about being underground and surrounded by unconscious people.

One day, this could be me. I shiver.

Most fae fall dormant at some point in their long lives, but the idea of it gives me hives. Perhaps because I'm young. Perhaps because dormancy has stolen my mother from me. Perhaps because the very idea of being stuck inside a closed cradle makes my stomach flip and my throat clench.

A couple of deep breaths help me relax my shoulders and clear my mind as I sit on the bench in front of her cradle.

"Hello, Mother." I run my finger along her name on the

plaque. Elara Greywind. "Happy birthday. I brought you something."

I place the flowers from the street boy at her feet. At least I hope that's where her feet are. If I've been talking to her feet instead of her head all these years, I'm going to feel so dumb.

"I know you can't see them, but they're the most beautiful flowers from the south. They smell sweet as candy, and the colors are orange, purple, and green. I'm wearing one in my hair as well, an orange one to match my eyes. Are your eyes orange as well? Did mine come from you? Because Father's are gray, so they didn't come from him.

"He says 'hello,' by the way." That's a lie. He doesn't send messages to Mother through me. I don't know if he visits her because he won't talk about her, and he complains when I do. "And so does Rahz." This is true. Rahz always sends his goodwill when he doesn't accompany me and can say as much himself. He'd have come with me today if I'd asked, but sometimes I like to make the trip alone. To have Mother all to myself.

"He's worried, you know." She doesn't, but who cares? What else am I supposed to talk about? "There's talk of fighting in the south. An uprising. Can you believe it? In Luminia? But we're peaceful here, so the talk may still prove false. But the chatter worries Rahz. He's always quick to fret."

I straighten my legs, cross my ankles, and wiggle my toes in the borrowed sandals. I'm twitchier than normal today. The urge to make this a short visit is hard to ignore, but I find it important my mother knows my voice. Whether she hears me or not, whether she remembers me or not, I have little control, but I owe her my best effort.

So I stay. And I talk. I tell her everything, all my secrets and wishes. The stone bench warms beneath my bottom as I rattle off whatever comes to mind. I don't leave until my throat is dry and my thirst demands I seek water.

Before going, I cast a quick look behind me to make sure we're still alone. Confirming as much, I lean in, resting my weight against the weight of her in the cradle. This is forbidden. One mustn't try to wake a dormant fae or disturb them in any way. But I'm so careful. So gentle. I'm not trying to wake her before she's ready. I just want to feel her against me a little bit, to take comfort in her closeness for the span of a few stolen heartbeats.

"Until next time, Mother. I love you. Rest well."

I kiss the fine pink silk of the cradle at shoulder level, and then I take my leave.

Chapter Seven

~Six Months Later~

Rahz

My mother paces the length of our tiny kitchen in the guise of putting away dishes. "What does it mean?" Anxiety has crept into her tone like fog along the horizon. "Register for what?" She runs a hand over her glossy brown hair, slicked back into a bun so as not to get in her way when she heads to work later.

I haven't wrapped my head around the news either and don't know what to say to calm her fears. "Not sure."

The weather has begun to warm. Spring is in the air. Seedlings are sprouting, flower blossoms are putting on a show, and a delegation from the royal family has just made their annual trip through Jodpirn. Gilded royal carriages trailing silk banners and topped with golden fringed canopies look so out of place here among the farms, but I saw them with my own eyes. Heard the news with my own ears.

Usually, their visit brings good tidings from our queen and her consort, perhaps a stash of candied treats from Lemossin's fine cooks, and news of the realm. In return, our regional anax contributes a tithe and several cartfuls of provisions, makes our reports, and shares word of births, deaths, and dormancies. It's generally a quick visit. We're but one small stop along their route that circumnavigates the continent. Nothing noteworthy has come from the annual visit since the youngest princess was born, and even that, though joyous, barely affected us out here in the countryside.

Mother clinks the last of the dishes away, drops into the chair next to mine, and puts her hand on my knee. "Maybe you shouldn't."

I'm thinking the same thing. "But they say it's mandatory."

"How will they know?" Her brown eyes shine with intensity. "If they need you to register, it means they don't have an accurate count of mixlings to begin with. They're trying to establish one. And what is a pledge but words spoken one day that can surely be revoked the next? It's better they don't keep track of you."

My breakfast isn't sitting well, with my stomach tied in knots. Mother's fretting doesn't help, though I'm inclined to agree with her. The delegation's thinly veiled command for all mixlings to make the trip to Lemossin, register their ancestry, and pledge their allegiance to the fae queen and her consort bristles the hair on my nape. I need to talk to Jindal. He'll know what to say to calm me down.

I place my hand on my mother's and squeeze. A sense of her unease washes over me with the contact. "Well, I don't have to do anything yet. There's a four-month window in which to make the trip, so we can afford to think on it."

"I have a bad feeling about this. First the news of fighting in the south, talk of an uprising, and now Queen Aurielle requiring pilgrimages and pledges, but only from those of mixed heritage? Your grandparents are rolling over in their graves, Rahz. Especially my father. He always thought we'd be stronger if we united."

"What do you mean?" And what of my own father, I wonder, but I won't upset her further with the question. Speaking of him only serves to make her sad.

"Your grandfather was always quick to remind us we humans outnumber fae in Luminia," she explains. "We may have shorter lives, but we bear children much faster. We don't go dormant. He said if we ever chose to band together and demand better treatment, demand our equal share of resources, the fae would be forced to comply."

I shift in my seat. My memories of my grandfather are of a gentle, gray-haired old man who always had a spare piece of candy in his front pocket for me, a toothy smile on his face, and a sweet-smelling pipe in his hand. It's hard to picture him imagining some sort of revolution.

Mother continues, "I thought he was spouting nonsense. But I was young. The fae in our village were kind to me. Your father was kind to me. It was easy to overlook injustice when I was hardly affected by it. But now? Well, I'm older, and I'd like to think wiser. I find myself wondering if your grandfather was right all along."

Since she brought him up herself, I can't be expected to resist the topic. "My father was kind to you?"

Her laughter surprises me, cutting through the tense moment like the calm before a storm. "Of course he was, Rahz. What did you think? That I'd fall in love with a man who treated me poorly?"

I shrug. "I didn't know. You don't like to speak of him."

She reclaims her hand, crosses her arms, and leans back in her seat. A thoughtful, faraway expression graces her oval face.

It's easy to see the young beauty she must have been. Even now, in middle age, my mother is stunning. Big brown eyes, perfectly arched brows, dark hair, and cherubic plump cheeks. She has a strong build, her arms defined in lean muscle from years of working the soil, working to run our household, working to keep the other villagers happy. As a young woman, she'd have been something else. No wonder my father fell for her.

If only I could understand why he left.

"You're right." She sighs. "I don't. But perhaps I've been unfair to you in that. I don't want you to think poorly of a man you've never met, yet I don't want you to like him either. Selfish of me, isn't it?"

"You have your reasons."

"Do I?" Her gaze returns from the distance to focus on me. "What would you like to know, dear? This is as good a time as any."

I'm certainly not going to argue, but I fail to see her logic. I'm all worked up over the registry, riddled with worry that threatens to become fear, and though I've harbored unanswered questions about my father my entire life, now hardly seems the time for a calm discussion. But I won't let the rare opportunity slip past me. Bad timing or not, I'm going to ask.

"What happened, Mother? If you loved each other, why did it change? Why did he go?"

There. It's out of me and dangling between us like a dew drop from a petal. Destined to fall but somehow still beautiful in the light.

I can't imagine falling out of love. My feelings for Jindal are eternal. Nothing could change our bond.

Another sigh as she gathers herself. "I didn't know him as well as I thought I did. Liam was so much older, but with fae, you really can't tell by looking. And he was so handsome. I thought he'd given me his heart, but really he only ever gave me his attention. His heart, if he had one, was held back. Unknowable until it was too late."

"What do you mean?"

"There's a reason I don't speak of this." Her gaze bores into mine. I repress a shiver. "Rahz Starling, you mustn't blame yourself for Liam's failings. This has nothing to do with you, not really, and everything to do with his ugly prejudices. That much must be clear before I continue."

I appreciate her words, but if she thinks for one second I don't already know I'm the reason my father is gone, she's wrong. Of course I'm the reason. Until me, they were together. After, they were apart. What's the obvious difference?

But I don't want her to feel bad, so I offer the reassurance she needs to continue. "Of course. I was only a baby. Not my fault."

My fault, my fault, my fault.

"Good. You're a clever lad. Don't ever let anyone say otherwise." She takes a fortifying breath, and her story tumbles out in a hurry. As if the faster she says it, the less it will matter. "When I met him, Liam was an absolute dream. He doted on me. Offered gifts. Said sweet things. He was funny. Charming. A traveler with fascinating stories. He once made me a necklace of shells he'd found on a trip to the coast. Crafted the piece himself. Back then, I never took it off."

Her hand ghosts over the skin of her throat, touching the phantom necklace. Does she still have it tucked away somewhere? I've never seen a necklace of shells anywhere in our house.

"He was kind. Fun to be around. We got up to all sorts of mischief together, climbing the cliffs over at Redfern Gulley and swimming in Mirror Lake, even after the top layer had frozen over for winter. It's a wonder we weren't injured."

She shakes her head and casts her gaze down. "Some humans fall pregnant easily. I didn't know how easily. Liam didn't know it could happen at all, not unless he willed the babe to my belly, which he didn't, so he thought we were safe. I thought we were safe."

She pauses. I know she's trying to spare my feelings, but she shouldn't. She isn't to blame for my father's shortcomings.

"One morning, I woke up queasy. The feeling continued off and on each morning throughout the week. When my mother asked what was wrong, I told her. I'll never forget the look on her face. I asked, 'What is it? What's the matter?' She sat me down and asked about Liam. About what we'd gotten up to. Though my cheeks were burning, I spilled my secrets. Her eyes got so wide I thought they'd pop out of her head. She hadn't realized how far I'd gone with him. She said there were things I should know. Things she should've taught me sooner. Anyway, she knew then, and I came around to believe her shortly thereafter that I was with child. With you."

Mother pats my cheek. Her smile says she was happy with this news, but I think that must be easier some twenty-plus years after the fact. She must have been scared back then, even if she won't say as much now.

"It took me a few weeks to come to the same conclusion my mother did. To wrap my mind around the idea of a new life growing within me. I'd always imagined being a mother. As a young child, I carried around my dolls, pretending they were my children. I looked forward to motherhood, and though I was surprised at how fast it had happened, I was excited.

"I thought Liam would be excited too. When I was absolutely sure of the pregnancy, I planned a special dinner to break the news. Mother helped. I baked sweets. My father wasn't thrilled at first that the baby would be half fae—he never liked Liam—but he was eager for a grandchild."

Mother grows silent. My chest is tight. The reveal couldn't have gone well. I feel bad for asking her to relive it, but I'm also thankful she's finally willing. I don't rush her.

"Liam wasn't excited. In fact, he didn't even believe me. Fae children cannot happen without the combined will of both parents, and as he hadn't willed the pregnancy, he refused to believe it was real. Asked me for proof. Pointed to my flat belly in disbelief and called me a liar."

I'm angry on her behalf. My neck heats. My hands ball into fists of their own accord. How dare anyone call my mother a liar? She is no such thing. If I could go back in time and argue with my father, I would.

"I cried. My only proof was the changes within my body, not yet visible to the naked eye and far too personal to share with an angry man. We ate the dinner my mother and I had cooked in silence. I didn't enjoy the sweets I'd baked, the taste of his disbelief bitter on my tongue. He did apologize for making me cry and softened toward me as he tried to explain why I had to be wrong, but by then, the damage was done. He wasn't ready to be a father and wouldn't have chosen me to be the mother of his children, and I knew it."

A pang of hurt constricts my chest. I'd suspected as much, but it's still hard to hear. Harder still to see my mother's buried sorrow. She deserved better. She deserved the world.

"When the inevitable came to pass, and my situation became too obvious to ignore, Liam left. No well wishes, no kiss good-bye, just an empty house and a glaring absence at my side each time I was asked, 'Who's the father?'"

She gives me a warm look. "But it mattered little, for I already had a new love. The love of a lifetime, in fact. A love no one could steal away. Because I had my Rahz, and I knew we'd be okay."

I didn't plan on crying this morning. "Mumma," my boyhood name for her, escapes with a sigh, and I collapse into her open arms. I'm bigger than she is, but within the circle of her embrace, I still feel small and protected.

"I love you so much." She strokes my back. "And though I

was disappointed in Liam, I harbor no ill will. Not anymore. He gave me you."

I sniffle into the warm fabric of her apron, pulling myself together and sitting up. "I love you too, Mumma."

And I'm disappointed in Liam. What a slug he is to abandon my mother. To abandon me. To insist on being right, even when he was wrong. I'm glad I don't know him. Nothing about him seems like a person I'd want to know.

Besides, Mother is right. We have each other, and we're okay. And now we have Jindal too.

Jindal.

I have to tell him everything. The urge to barrel out of the house and to his side rises like a tidal wave.

Mother, as if sensing this, stands up, brushes off her skirts, and puts her hands on her hips. "Well, go on, then. I know you want to." Her eyes twinkle when she looks at me.

"You don't mind if I tell him?"

She laughs. Relief courses through me to see her jovial nature shine through even the most dramatic of mornings. "Never in a million years. I'm glad you and Jindal don't keep secrets from each other. It's a good thing."

I kiss her cheek. "Thank you, Mother."

"Come back tomorrow and tell me what he thinks of this registration and pledge business."

"I will."

The door sticks on my way out, swollen in its frame like it always is when the weather warms, reminding me that some things never change. I hurry to prepare Magna for a ride, eager to find Jindal, who's cloistered off with his father getting this season's crop into the ground while the temperature is perfect.

They won't have heard the news and won't be expecting anything more than the usual good tidings. I'll need a good excuse to steal Jindal away from his father today, and I have only the ten-minute ride to their place to think of one.

Chapter Eight

Jindal

THE SUN WARMS MY BACK, DIRT CLINGS UNDERNEATH my fingernails, and every seed gets a little whisper of my magic to help it along. All the makings of a wonderful day.

I love this time of year. Planting season. I love the harvest too, but there's something about a fresh beginning, a clean slate, and a tilled field full of potential that both energizes and calms me at once.

Father is working on our leafy greens section while I'm tending the beans. Long beans, purple runners, succotash, dragon tongues, and winged snake beans, all planted beneath the scattered shade of the trellis Rahz and I built together so they can climb as high as they want.

The telltale clomping of hooves catches my attention, and I glance up. Rahz is racing our way astride Magna.

What's got him in such a hurry?

I stand and stretch my body while he dismounts and loops Magna's reins over the fence. For a few seconds, he doesn't move, a distressed expression on his face. Something is wrong. Without a backward glance at my father—he'll disapprove of anything that pauses my work in our fields today—I trot over to Rahz to find out what's going on.

He meets me halfway. "Jin."

His eyes look sad. I reach for him, and he scoops me up. While this sort of greeting isn't unusual for us, the way he holds me feels different. Like I'm a lifeline and he's a drowning man.

"What's happened, Rahz?" I murmur against his neck, where my face is practically smooshed against his throat. "Why are you sad?"

He sets me down. "Can we go somewhere? The lake, maybe."

"Of course." Father won't like it, but I don't care. I'm too old now to be thrown across his lap for a spanking, and he can be mad all he likes. Won't be much different from any other day.

Rahz gathers Magna's reins, and we walk through the fields, past our cottage, and out of my father's hearing range.

"So what's the matter? I'm worried now."

"Where should I begin?"

He's not really asking me. He's sorting it out in his mind. I can tell by the look on his face, both thoughtful and troubled. I shift my gaze to the yellow buttercups dotting the ground ahead of us and give him the time he needs.

As we walk, a slow meandering amble, the story unfolds one shaky sentence at a time. First his mother's tale. Much of which we'd already expected. At least something along those lines, that is. We've done quite a lot of speculating over the years, as she's never spoken at length about Rahz's father before now. We knew he was fae, of course, and that he was gone but not dead, and that was it.

As he recounts his mother's words, I hold Rahz's hand, knowing he feels he's to blame for his father's absence. For the abandonment of his mother in her time of need. I also know there's nothing I can say to him in this moment to change his mind, but perhaps, over time, he'll understand it's not his fault.

Magna, too, senses his distress. She snuffles his hair, lipping the flowing silver locks and covering them in nose slime, which, at least, makes us both chuckle despite the somber mood.

By the time we reach the grassy banks of Mirror Lake, he's telling me of the royal delegation's visit, their fancy wagons, and their strange proclamations. With the flurry of activity spring planting entails, I'd all but forgotten they'd be passing through. But Rahz was in town with many of the other villagers to greet them, along with Jodpirn's representative, Anax Grippa.

"Wait, what?" I stop midstride. "They want us to go all the way to Lemossin to sign some fancy piece of paper?"

"Not 'us,' Jin, only mixlings of human heritage. I don't pretend to understand, but it can't be good. And not just to sign the registry but also to make loyalty pledges to the royal family."

Thinking this over, I kick off my shoes. Rahz releases Magna to drink from the lake and eat her fill of grass, trusting her to stick around. Or at least to return when he whistles. He takes off his shoes as well. In unspoken agreement, we wade into the cool water. Our feet sink into the mud. I like the goopy muck of it squishing between my toes.

"Maybe it's not bad," I offer. "Maybe they're only making sure mixlings know they're valued just as much as full fae."

He scoffs. "You can't possibly believe that."

My gut lurches. I can't deny my feelings are a little bruised by the harshness seeping into his tone, but I know he doesn't mean anything by it. He's stressed. And he's received the emotional blow of a lifetime this morning, so I let it pass.

"It could be true." My voice comes out small and low.

He rolls his eyes. "But we clearly aren't as valued. Take me, for example. You saw what I went through in school before my magic developed. What my mom goes through day in and day out. It isn't fair."

Words fail me. We were all picked on in school; it's what kids do. Sure, maybe Rahz got it worse because Vander took an early disliking to him, but it was only teasing. And Rahz's mother has always seemed happy to me. Quick to smile, with a cheerful disposition and a kind word for anyone who crosses her path. What's Rahz referring to? What does he mean?

I open my mouth to ask when he says with a vehemence uncommon to his usual patter, "I'm not going. I won't sign their registry, and I won't pledge my loyalty to Aurielle."

My jaw drops. "What? You aren't loyal to our queen? But why, when she has provided so much? I don't understand."

He spins, his expression fierce. "What has she provided, exactly? What? Not our shelter—we built that ourselves—not the fertile soil, which rightly belongs to all creatures, not the food on our plates or the clothes on our backs. We provided that. *Our* work. I owe her nothing, least of all my name on a registry declaring my human heritage, my magical powers, my age, my hometown. What could she possibly need that information for that benefits me?"

I blink, overwhelmed. My stomach knots. Rahz speaks with such force I feel we're in an argument, and I don't want to argue. But I must disagree. "The queen ensures our realm's safety. She keeps the peace. She protects our history, the light lineages, the—"

"What peace? The one where fae can come and go as they please, work or not work while humans pick up the slack to keep the cities running? And mixlings like me fall somewhere in between, not a true member of either group? What protection? What is she protecting us from, exactly?"

I'm stunned. His doubts hit like a jolt to my heart, speeding it up a notch. In my failure to reply, he shakes his head. Is he disappointed in me?

Rahz walks farther into the lake until the water dampens his pants, where he's rolled them up to the knee. I stay where I am, carefully turning over all he said. A sinking feeling lodges in my gut.

I trust the royal family, even if Rahz doesn't. It's what I've been taught. All I know. Our comfort, our happiness, and all the abundance in our lives are because the four light lineages—including Aurielle and her consort—protect the realm.

Why would they lie? And what would they have to gain from Rahz's name on a registry? Nothing I can think of. Meanwhile, perhaps such a thing would finally make him feel included. Like he belongs. Because he does. But that's not how he's interpreting things at all.

A large swath of gently rippling water separates us. I watch the flow as my thoughts run wild. What should I say? How can I help?

Before a solution hits me, Rahz sinks into the water's depths, clothes and all, leaving only a splash where his feet kick, propelling him farther away from me and churning the water between us.

It's far too cold to be swimming for my liking, so I don't follow. The unbroken surface of the lake glimmers in the midday sunlight. I pick a spot, guessing that's where he'll emerge, and stare at it.

But I'm wrong. When his head breaks the surface, I see he went in the opposite direction. He flings his hair back, creating a sparkling arc of droplets cascading high over his shoulders. He's lovely to look at, as always, but my heart hurts for him. He's torn, and I haven't helped.

Somehow I feel as though I've made things worse.

Rahz catches my gaze, his eyes blazing like wildfire. Heat despite the crisp water of early spring. He stalks toward me, and the mood shifts.

Oh.

A swell of anticipation quickens my heart. This is often how we handle our problems.

"Jin." My name is desire from his lips. With every step he takes forward, I shuffle back, out of the water, and onto the riverbank.

I like the way he looks at me. His intensity. As always, my body responds to him, cock filling, belly tingling. I'm ready to give him whatever he wants.

He strips his wet clothes off as he nears. "Do you want—"

"Yes." There's no need to finish that question. "Anything. I want." I'm unbuttoning my shirt when he grabs the laces of my pants and deftly works them free.

This will always bring us back to each other. This connection. This magnetism that smolders without end. An irresistible force we feed often and with enthusiasm.

When we are naked and kissing, skin to skin, we forget the disagreement. At least I do. He lifts me off my feet and, with magic and muscle combined, deposits me on my back in the thick grass. I whisper my own bit of magic to the plants, the soil, the ground beneath, and they cushion us without getting us dirty. These little tricks we learned early, anything to facilitate our rising need for each other.

I'm parting my legs for him, but he shakes his head and manhandles me to my stomach. Yes. I love it when he gets like this, taking what he needs. My mind hazes over as my body gives way to his pleasure.

His fingers dance along my spine, run over my wings to the tips and back down. I shiver. This time he doesn't stop me when I open my legs and tilt my hind end for him, asking for what I want with every movement. Showing him I'm ready.

His touch travels lower to the place I've eagerly revealed to him, and lingers.

I moan, pressing back. "Give it to me. Take me."

Slick fingers trace my rim, but I don't think either of us is patient enough for a slow and steady preparation. I want it hard. Now.

"Rahz, don't tease."

It's all the permission he needs. Fingers are replaced by his cock, hot and heavy, as he pushes past my body's feeble resistance and enters me.

He stretches me wide and fills me, his groan of pleasure music to my ears. I clench my fists around two clumps of grass and grit my teeth.

"You feel so good." He drops his weight onto my back and wraps his arms beneath me, gathering me in a strong hold. I tear the grass up by the roots as my arms are pinned to my sides by his embrace.

I can hardly move, but I don't have to. He's doing all the work for both of us, his hips driving me farther into the ground with every thrust. All I have to do is lie here and take it—his cock pounding my insides until I'm buzzing with the need to come, his chest trapping my wings between us, his teeth biting a chunk of muscle in my shoulder.

I squeal my delight, so drowned by sensations I don't know whether to beg him to keep going or beg him to stop. I love it. I hope it never ends. I hope he comes in my ass. I hope I spill without even touching my cock.

"Can you take more?" he murmurs in my ear. My brain latches on to the meaning, and I moan my assent. He pauses, and somehow the stillness is more intense than the movement. "Is that a yes?"

"Yes, yes, yes." Anything to make him keep going. To fuck me into oblivion.

Rahz is normally a tender lover. Thoughtful. Thorough. Giving. And I appreciate that; I do. But this? Right now? This raw need and desperate coupling? I'm losing my mind it's so good.

"Fuck me harder."

His teeth return to my shoulder, and he does as I say. For one breathless heartbeat, I almost regret it. He slams into me so hard

I squeeze my eyes closed, and stars explode behind the lids. But then it's good again. Better than good. Electrifying, like a light storm snapping and sizzling in the air of a hot summer's night.

My muscles tense. Rahz grips me tighter. Our bodies draw pleasure with a wicked hint of pain from each other in a spiraling loop of rapture.

I'm going to come. There's no holding back the rush of euphoria as it hits. My poor, leaking cock is trapped between me and the ground, but I'm going to come anyway. My body is already shuddering in Rahz's embrace. But I don't want to be first.

"Need you." The words punch out with his thrusts. "Come with me. Rahz, please."

"Anything for you." He answers with words and action. His cock swells twice in size in a matter of seconds, stretching me to the limit, pounding so far into me I feel it in my throat.

When I can't hold out a second longer, my body gives itself up completely. So does his. We peak together, shaking, panting, moaning. His cock pulses inside me while mine spurts hot and sticky under my belly. I vibrate with the pleasure of it, Rahz and I, joined as one.

Whatever happens, we'll always have this.

As we catch our breath, the sun slips behind a cloud, and the cool shade is a welcome respite from the heat we created.

Rahz loosens his grip, kisses my shoulder, and eases us to our sides. He stays in me, and I'm glad. It's too soon to lose this connection. I need more time. Always more time.

He trails a hand down my belly and caresses my spent cock. It's a lot. I'm so sensitive there now. Overly so. But I don't squirm away. I want his hand on me.

He rubs my cum in little circles around my slit and presses messy little kisses against the back of my neck. I'm floating in sensation, ass open wide, body limp as a rag, mind perfectly at peace. Rahz never fails to produce this effect in me. To give me this. Hopefully, I'm giving as much to him in return. I want to.

I'm nearly asleep when his body slips from mine, and I mourn the loss. He stays curled around me, though, holding me to his chest.

He whispers in my ear, "So sweet for me, Jin. Such a minx. Can't get enough of you."

My lips curl to a smile at his praise. "You can have more of me whenever you're ready." I wiggle my ass against his spent cock, eliciting a sexy groan from him against my ear.

"Perhaps I'll take you up on that." He gives my nipple a light pinch. "Later."

I bite my cheek, hoping he does. I don't want anything to do with reality for the rest of the day. No mysterious registries, no news from the royal court, no dormant mothers or absent fathers, just Rahz and me, and this feeling of being united against the world. Forever.

Chapter Nine

RAHZ

WITH THE RISING OF THIS MONTH'S ROUND MOON, our old group, plus a few new members, meet down at Redfern Gulley. Though we no longer get together at every single round moon like we did when we were children, neither have we let these gatherings become rare. We meet four, maybe five times a year, when someone bothers to plan, when there's something to be celebrated or something to be mourned. When the mood strikes.

And the mood has struck like a lightning bolt—bright, bold, and urgent.

A certain restlessness cropped up among us in the weeks since the royal delegation's visit and brought with it an implicit understanding that we'd gather this month.

The round moon's silver light casts a hazy glow over the gulley as Jindal and I trundle down the switchbacks to the rocky ledge about halfway down. On the other side of the giant gulley is a sheer cliff, the same one my mother said she'd climbed with my father in her youth. He would have had wings to ensure his safety, but my mother? She'd have had to free-climb.

Crazy woman. I'll stick to the safety of the worn path, thank you very much.

It's windy tonight, the breeze blowing my hair around enough to make me wish I'd tied it back like Jindal's. His purple curls are secured with a black leather band at his nape. Already I look forward to pulling that band loose and freeing his hair to spill down his back later tonight.

I carry a shoulder bag with two jugs of cherry ale, which clink together despite the towel I shoved between them. Jindal has a basket of Bessa's pastries to share. He could fly, of course, but he walks by my side instead, and for that, I'm grateful. My nerves keep me on edge, and his presence is a balm.

How will the others view the royal decree? What will they expect of me when even Jindal doesn't understand my reluctance to sign a mixling registry?

Not that he isn't trying. Jindal is always willing to lend an ear, to hear me out when my thoughts wander aloud. He knows I worry about an underlying meaning, about a potential conflict, about the war still raging in my night terrors. But he's stubborn in his belief we're safe here. That the fae court will always ensure the peace no matter what.

But we're both quick to find more pleasurable things to do with each other than squabble.

So while I continue to prepare for the worst, if only in my mind, Jindal carries on as if nothing is wrong.

I don't blame him for it. Perhaps I could be more direct. More insistent. But what's the use of convincing him to worry when I do it enough for both of us?

Even still, I want to know what the others have to say.

When we arrive, Salah and Lemon, with their mates, twin brothers Arrow and Wilder, are already seated on fallen logs long since maneuvered into a circle. The twins are from Clodhill and met the sisters during our local Gatherdawn a few cycles back. The four of them have been inseparable ever since.

I hate to admit it, but the only way to tell one twin from the other is by which sister they're doting on. Otherwise, their looks are indistinguishable. Glimmering mulberry-colored skin, minty green hair and wings, yellow eyes topped with dancing bushy eyebrows they each use like beacons to express what they're feeling. Nice guys. Friendly, silly, fun. I'm happy Salah and Lemon found them. And I'm glad they were the first to arrive. Greeting them is easy. Hugs all around as Jindal and Lemon spread the food on the low stone boulder we use as a table.

"I've brought berries and sweet cakes," says Lemon. "You?"

"Bessa's apricot pastries, of course." Jindal holds up a silver tin. "She wouldn't let Rahz go without his favorite on the round moon."

"Sweet Bessa." Lemon snags a pastry. "We're lucky to have her."

Bringing my flame magic to my fingertips, I light a floating fire at the center to keep us warm. It sparks to life, orange and red dancing blazes flickering and popping just like a real fire, but this one is harmless. It won't burn anything unless I direct it to, and even the night's gusty winds can't blow it astray.

"Show off." Vander's voice, from up the path, grating, as usual. We get along now. Mostly. We have to. We're members of the same village and must work together often. But I'll never like him. After all these years, he still finds a way to get under my skin with only a few words.

"Oh, shut up, Vander." Jindal comes to my defense, also as usual. "Unless you'd rather do it yourself or have us all freeze our buns off all night long."

The others, except for Lemon, couldn't maintain the fire as effortlessly as I can. Cast it, maybe, but not keep it going without expending enough effort to tire them out and exhaust their magic. Vander won't admit as much, but we all know it makes the most sense for me to provide the fire. The effort is so minimal I barely notice.

As the others arrive—Basil and Petzyl, together as always, then Jord and Cindra, and finally Nellie and Bird with Bird's new beau Falen—pleasantries and chitchat grow louder and more excited. It's nice when we can all get together like this. Like the old days.

I'm glad for Falen's presence in our group. He's the only other mixling, and though his fae features are much more prominent than mine, including a set of shimmery, flightless, opalescent wings on his back, his human heritage is also obvious. He's nearly as tall as me, with a broader form than most fae, chocolate-brown eyes, and brown hair to match. There's no denying the characteristics of either race in his features, whereas aside from my pointed ears and silver hair, I'm as human-looking as they come.

Like me, Falen will be required to make the pilgrimage to Lemossin to sign his name on the registry. He'll be asked to pledge his loyalty to Queen Aurielle and her consort, Lord Warner. I've been meaning to steal a few minutes with him to ask his thoughts on the matter, but with the planting season upon us, we've been too busy to carve out time for socializing.

We're gathered in a circle around the fire, drinking cherry ale and eating from a platter of cheeses, dried fruits, olives, and sweets when the topic we're all anticipating comes around.

Vander is looking straight at me when he asks, "What did they tell you about the new registry? And why do they only want your kind? What about the rest of us?"

Trust Vander to want to be included in something, even if that something is shadier than a dark alleyway at midnight on the Samuin.

Because he's watching me, so do the others. I hadn't wanted to share my thoughts first, but it would be even more awkward to stay silent.

My tongue feels thick in my mouth. "I know only as much as you do."

"But you were in the village during the pronouncement." Vander pushes. "What did they say?"

I take a swig of my ale, trying to maintain a casual air, as if I hadn't been fretting over the what-ifs around this subject for weeks. "Only what you've already heard from the countless others who were there. I have no new information, same as you."

Does he think I attended some secret meeting of mixlings he wasn't privy to? We don't have those. And if we did, Vander would already know it. He's got his nose in everything.

Lemon clears her throat. "Our father spoke with Anax Grippa Sunday last. He says the royal party was very tight-lipped about the whole thing. Strikes me as odd. They usually love to hear themselves talk."

"Do you think it has to do with the humans stirring up trouble in the south?" asks Basil. He and Petzyl sit shoulder to shoulder, crossing their legs toward each other in a mirror image. If Basil thinks the humans have something to do with it, you can bet Petzyl does as well. I wouldn't be surprised if it turns out they share the same brain.

Jindal leans in closer to me. "But those are only rumors."

Vander is quick to shake his head. "Not rumors. There's fighting in the southern region. My father has spoken with his cousin, who has business from Lemossin to Irondale. Violence has broken out in the streets. Humans attacking fae. And when the fae fought back, the humans were forced into hiding. The southernmost trade routes are compromised."

My breath stalls in my throat. Jindal hooks our elbows and squeezes.

As much as I dislike Vander, his information is usually trustworthy. He comes from a long line of traveling merchants and, as such, has family scattered all around Luminia. They always seem to know what's going on before the rest of us. No wonder he's curious about the registry. He isn't used to having unanswered questions.

I'm not the only one at a loss for words. Jaws are dropping left and right. My gaze shifts to Falen, who shifts uncomfortably in his spot next to Bird.

"Did anyone die?" asks Salah, her face stricken.

"I don't know, though enough blood has been spilled to declare the area dangerous to travelers. So far, the trouble is contained in Irondale, but already some fae are migrating north. An influx arrived in Willowood just last week. Great for business. They left much of their belongings back home and had to buy all new things. They say staying wasn't worth the risk. Too many humans in Irondale, not enough fae."

So it's true. It's happening. An uprising, just like my grandfather had imagined. A wave of fear prickles the hair on my nape as the howl of the wind through the pines above us roars louder.

"But what has that got to do with the mixling registry?" Bird presses her lips to a worried thin line. What conversations have she and Falen had about this? Are they anything like what Jindal and I have been discussing?

Or very carefully not discussing.

Basil answers, "I don't know anything for sure, but it makes sense the queen would want to shore up loyalty among the halfbre—er, mixlings. If it comes to fighting, it's better to have them on our side than on the humans'."

And there it is. The heart of the matter.

Will I be expected to choose sides? Is that what this is? Though it's what I've feared since my nightmares began all those years ago, hearing it aloud makes the looming possibility all the more real.

I am both human and fae, yet I'm also neither, but more important than that, I don't wish to fight.

Falen's voice is gentle when he speaks. Our gazes meet over

his words. "When will you go to Lemossin, Rahz? Shall we make the journey together?"

Jindal stiffens next to me. Perhaps it's finally becoming real to him too. If I'm to make this trip, I'll need to leave him for a time. We can't both go. There's too much to be done here in Jodpirn for us to leave together. The animals to care for, the crop to grow, the chores to be done. Not that his father would let him leave anyway. Had he really not thought of this part?

"I don't know when." In truth, I hoped not to go at all, but I don't see an easy way out of it, not if the town expects it of me. "But I would welcome your company, yes."

"Maybe you shouldn't," Lemon blurts. "I mean, how will they even know if you don't?"

"We'll know," says Vander. His tone holds the hint of a threat.

"So what? What do you care what Rahz and Falen do?" Lemon counters, and I love her all the more for saying the things I cannot.

"It's a royal decree." Vander's ale sloshes in his mug as he gestures a little too enthusiastically for my liking. "To deny the order is to commit treason."

Treason.

Is that what I'd be doing? The word sounds so serious for such a small act. To sign or not to sign. To declare or not to declare. Not making the journey to Lemossin doesn't feel like it should be a crime.

Vander continues, his voice drowning out a low rumble of thunder in the distance. "What's the problem? You *are* loyal to our queen, aren't you?"

No. I'm decidedly not. I have nothing against the woman, but I don't know her. I owe her nothing.

"Yes," says Falen without hesitation. "Though you must agree, making the trip to Lemossin is a hassle. Round and back will take a month at least and require quite a bit of coin for the journey. Inns, horses, food. It's a lot to ask."

Thankfully, he answered so that I don't have to. Jindal's orange gaze studies my face. What's he thinking?

"Why couldn't the royal delegation have brought the cursed thing here when they passed through?" asks Salah.

The twin next to her, Arrow, I think, adds, "Yeah. If it's just a fancy piece of parchment to sign, why not make it easier for the mixlings to do?"

Why, indeed? It hadn't occurred to me they might be gathering us to the capital for some other more nefarious reason, but now that it has, I won't be able to banish the fear from my mind. I hope that's not the case.

"I don't want to go," I admit. "My work is here, and so is Jindal."

"I don't see that you have a choice," says Vander, which is quite unnecessary after the whole *treason* comment earlier.

Jindal curls closer to my side. His silence is odd. He's usually my little chatterbug.

"You could bring Jindal with you," says Bird. "If we can make the extra coin in time, I'm going to tag along with Falen. I've never been to Lemossin." Her sweet, encouraging smile is lovely, but Jin and I don't have the coin to spare. Nor the time to try to make any extra. Nor the extra set of hands on the farm, even if we had the money.

"I want him to stay." Jindal's words come out softly. He speaks like this when he's deep in thought. I'm both relieved and saddened that the gravity of the situation finally seems to be hitting him. I squeeze his arm in the crook of mine, relishing the warmth of him beside me as the wind further chills the air. If it weren't for the fire, we'd be shivering.

I turn the subject back to the revolt, trying to get more information out of Vander while I have the chance. "What did the humans cite as their reason for the violence? Did your cousin say anything else?"

Vander shrugs as if this part isn't important, whereas to me, it's the crux. "Too much work, not enough pay. Poor conditions." He waves this off. "Just lazy if you ask me. Everyone's got to pitch in. That's just life."

Easy for him to say. Vander does merely a fraction of the work I do around this town. My magical capabilities make it easier, so I don't mind taking on the additional responsibility. But for Vander to call others lazy pushes buttons I didn't realize I had. He is the laziest of our group, surely.

Must be nice, having the wealth of a family of merchants behind you, throwing coin at problems instead of actual work.

"There's too many of them," says Vander, and a chill grips my spine. "And they're too busy making more babies to get their share of the work done. They'll be sorry when the queen rallies fae troops. Numbers will never win over magic."

The iciness spreads so intensely I tremble. Jindal's gaze finds mine, and the worry in his eyes mirrors my own. He shifts closer.

How many of them think like Vander and are too polite to say so in mixed company? How many do not? I have my guesses as to which are which, but it's unnerving not to know for certain.

The stuff of my nightmares flashes in my mind's eye. War. Humans against fae. Suffering. Death. Blood.

"Troops?" Bird's voice has gone shrill. "You think the queen will raise an army?"

Falen encircles her waist with a comforting arm. "Surely it won't come to that."

"Don't know," says Vander. "But she should. Squash the rebellion in its tracks. Manage the population. Keep the peace."

"Manage the population?" Asks the twin next to Lemon, probably Wilder.

"You can't keep the peace by murdering people," says the twin next to Salah, probably Arrow. It really is hard to tell.

Vander raises his brows but thankfully, keeps his mouth shut.

Bessa's apricot pastries have gone sour in my stomach. There's not enough cherry ale in Jodpirn for where this conversation is headed. I'd expected disagreement, opposing opinions, but talk of war as if it's reasonable to think such an event is on the horizon? I could've gone my whole life without that.

And yet...the fear is no longer solely my own. At least we are together in this.

Some of us.

The fire crackles and snaps, warming our fronts even while our backs grow chilly as the temperature plunges. For a moment, no one speaks. Each of us reflects in our own way. I take comfort in Jindal, tucked in under my arm as close as he can get without climbing into my lap. I feel his ribs expand on every inhale and contract on every exhale, and if I concentrate on that, things don't seem so bad.

Another rumble echoes from overhead, louder this time, tugging me out of my thoughts. Thunder this close? Normally, I'd have sensed bad weather approaching. I thought it would miss us. I must be even more distracted than I'd realized.

"Is that a storm coming?" Bird's wings flutter and resettle. "I don't like storms."

"Sounds like it." Petzyl glances at Basil on his side. "Maybe we should call it an early night?"

Basil nods. Another boom sounds, followed by the hissing crack and flash of lightning.

Everyone startles. Salah and Lemon rush to the stone table to clear up the food. The swoosh of approaching rain sweeps through the gulley.

I stuff what's left of the jugs of ale into my sack as Jindal gathers the pastries.

"Too bad you can't fly." Vander bumps his shoulder against mine. If he meant to shove me, it didn't work. He may be the bully, but I'll always be bigger. If he meant it to be friendly, yeah, I'll believe that when nillyslugs learn to gallop.

"That's fine." I shift my gaze from Vander to Falen, who can't fly either. "Falen and I can walk together."

"And me," says Jindal. "I'll walk with you."

Falen kisses Bird's cheek and assures her he'd rather she hurry home with the others before she can make the same offer. "I'll join you shortly."

I turn to say the same to Jindal, but he's shaking his head. "I'm with you."

Gathering his hand in mine, I tug him to the side. "I'd rather you fly." Voice lowered to a whisper, I say in his ear, "I want to speak with Falen alone. I think he wants the same. Please?"

Jindal's expression crumples, and his shoulders droop. He doesn't understand, but I'll explain it to him later. If we're alone, Falen can speak freely with me about this, something he's unlikely to do in the presence of a full-blooded fae he's only just begun to know. But Jindal's pout breaks my heart. "Rahz?"

Another loud clap of thunder pierces our eardrums. Storms that crop up out of nowhere tend to do the most damage.

"Please, Jin? Go with the others and hurry home safely. I'll be along soon."

His sad little nod tests my resolve, but I won't let this opportunity slide. Falen is the only one who might understand what I'm going through. We need to talk.

Jindal leaves with the others, buddying up with Bird, who's already taken to the sky. They'll be home in mere minutes, whereas the walk will take Falen and me at least a half hour.

Plenty of time to see if he's as willing to pledge his loyalty to the queen as he seems.

Chapter Ten

Jindal

By the time I arrive at our little hayloft in the barn, I'm blinking back tears. Not only because Rahz wanted to speak to Falen without me, which I can almost understand, but because of, well, everything.

I've done such a good job sticking my head in the sand that I'm only now realizing we'll be parted. For an entire month.

Perhaps even longer.

We've never been apart for more than a few nights in years. I don't sleep well without him when I know he's only one town over in Clodhill. So how will we manage the vast span of sunstrides between Jodpirn and Lemossin?

How will I know if he's safe?

My stomach churns, and my nerves are on edge. I hug myself, trying to sit still. Pacing won't help the time pass by any quicker.

Outside, the storm rages, banging the shutters on the house across the field, whistling through the rafters of the barn, pelting a deluge of rain that hopefully won't prove too much for the young seedlings we're growing. Rahz and Falen will be soaked through and chilled to the bone on their walk.

With that in mind, I light our biggest lantern. Real fire, not safe like Rahz's, but the kind that could light up this hayloft in seconds if I'm not careful. But it won't. Because I am careful. The little space around our bed feels warmer already. I collect a towel for him to dry his skin, some soft clothes to sleep in, and our coziest blankets to warm him up.

As I prepare, my mind turns over the night's conversation relentlessly, picking apart every word, every question.

I couldn't help but notice, when asked, Rahz didn't answer if he was loyal to our queen. I've always thought Aurielle is a good ruler and deserves our allegiance, but... Why would Rahz feel otherwise? Because his blood is only half fae? That doesn't make sense. We live in Luminia, forever ruled by the fae. She's his queen as much as mine. Why wouldn't he pledge his loyalty?

The questions disturb me on a night I already find myself very much disturbed. My thoughts are scattered like dandelion fluff on the wind. A sense of urgency whispers that time is running out, that I need to act before something important slips through my fingers, but I can't latch on to the answer.

I'll support Rahz. Of course I will. But it's difficult when I don't understand his reluctance. He's careful with what he tells me these days. As though his trust has limits. Boundaries he won't cross. Even with me. Though at this very moment he's telling Falen things while keeping me out.

I won't pretend my feelings aren't a little black and blue around the edges.

When Rahz makes it home, I've worked myself into a frenzy. The tears I'd held at bay slide down my cheeks. My face must be a mess. But he's drenched, and I'd planned on helping.

So I wipe my nose on my sleeve and grab the towel I'd dug out for this reason. I peer down at him from my spot in the loft.

"I'll just undress here," he says. "No sense bringing all these wet clothes to bed."

Not trusting myself to answer lest he realize my sad, pathetic state a moment earlier than necessary, I hover as he peels off the soaked layers. So beautiful, my Rahz. Naked, he hangs each piece on a separate rung to dry, then makes his way up.

Seconds tick by. I bite back shame at having come so undone while merely waiting for him for half an hour. The wooden rungs creak as they bear his weight. My heart beats too fast. My breath comes in too shallow.

I'm clutching the towel to my chest. Why does he even put up with me?

"Hey there." His voice cuts through the dark cloud I'm lost in, his expression shifting from neutral to concerned. "Jinny, love, what's wrong?" He wraps his arms around me and holds me tight to his damp skin.

I sniffle. I'm overreacting and yet unable to stop. I release the towel and cling to him, trapping it between us.

"Has something happened?" he murmurs in my hair.

How can I tell him nothing happened? Nothing except he walked home with someone else? Even I know that's not the real reason I'm crying, or not the only reason, but I don't have words for the feelings swirling inside me. Like my thoughts are too big for my body.

Rahz rubs my back, patient as ever. Sweet man.

"I don't want you to leave," I manage. Of the list of things that are bothering me, that concern is at the very top.

"And I don't want to go, but I don't see a way out of it. Not if the town expects me to make the trip." His sigh ruffles my hair. "If Vander thinks not signing the registry is an act of treason, he won't be the only one. He's just bold enough to say it out loud. It's dangerous to let the villagers believe I might not sign."

Dangerous. He's right. But it's crazy. Jodpirn has never been dangerous. *We're safe here, we're safe here, we're safe here*, my mind insists, but the truth hits me.

I might be safe, but Rahz isn't. And that's unacceptable.

Instead of diminishing, my tears run like a river overflowing its banks after a storm. I gulp in a shaky breath, and Rahz holds me closer. Together we rock, back and forth, back and forth, while I cry it out.

This isn't what I wanted to happen. I should be drying him off, tending to his hair, dressing him in soft clothes, asking how his conversation went.

"I thought maybe you were having a tough time tonight," he says. "I should've known how badly this was affecting you. I'm sorry I left you alone, but you're okay. I've got you."

His voice soothes my nerves but not my guilt. "Not your fault. You've been trying to tell me, haven't you? And I've been a terrible listener."

"You weren't ready."

A pitiful little laugh escapes my lips. "I'm still not. Clearly."

His laughter echoes mine, just as pitiful. "Aww, Jin. You're doing fine. Cry as much as you need."

Oddly, this helps the tears stop. I gather myself and take a deep breath, pulling back to look into his eyes. His warm, mossy-green, intelligent eyes. "Sorry."

Rahz swipes my wet cheeks with his thumbs. "No need."

I rescue the towel crumpled between us and run it over his wet hair. Rivulets trail over his collarbones and down his chest. One droplet finds a home for itself in his navel. He stays still while I dry him, even the drop in his belly button. Though a naked Rahz will always be a temptation, I hand over the clothes I readied for him and watch him dress in the soft, warm sleep shirt I laid out for him.

We slide into bed, and he puts out the fire with a wave of his hand. "Do you think we could talk about it, or do you need to sleep?"

"Talk. Definitely talk." I've already put this conversation off for far too long.

"Good." He kisses my nose.

We lie on our sides, facing each other. A common position for us and one that brings comfort. Even in the dark, I see his face clearly, knowing I'm in shadows for him. My eyesight is better. A boon in times like these when I can read him like a book, but he can only make out my shape. And yet another advantage of my blood that I didn't earn.

The rain pounds upon the metal roof overhead, nature's drumbeat. That, too, is soothing. Perhaps I'm ready for this conversation after all. "Tell me of your talk with Falen. Does he feel as you do? And what is that, by the way? How do you feel? I've been turning a blind eye long enough."

A faint smile lifts Rahz's pretty mouth. "Thank you for asking."

It's hard not to kiss him, but I resist. Can't get distracted now, even if it would be infinitely more fun.

"I don't want to sign the registry. And I certainly don't want to pledge my loyalty to anyone, save you, of course. But I don't see a way around at least making the trip. I'd thought, perhaps, Falen would feel as I do, but his reluctance stems more from the inconvenience of the task and less from what's actually being asked of us."

If only Falen had agreed with Rahz. I don't quite understand it all, but at least he'd have another person on his side. Rahz deserves that.

"Falen has been to Lemossin several times. His family cele-brated the Gatherdusk there when he was a boy. He remembers the royal court. Aurielle on horseback, parading through the city streets in all her glory. He listened to their speeches and dined upon feasts provided by the crown. It has inspired a sense of loyalty in him that I don't feel."

I don't want to interrupt, but my mind provides questions relentlessly. I tell it to shut up and listen for once instead.

Rahz twirls his fingers through my hair, lulling me to a calm, even as the world spins around me.

"Though we are both mixlings, Falen is more fae than I am in every way save blood. He's more at home in his fae skin. He even looks more fae than I do. His mother is fae, and his father is human, and they're happy together, unlike my parents. He's grown up feeling accepted."

In the quiet pause, I reflect that Rahz hasn't grown up feeling accepted, not completely, and my soul aches for his.

"He's comfortable. He doesn't know why Aurielle would ask him to sign a registry, but the request doesn't bother him. He's already loyal, so pledging himself thus hardly matters. But I can't stop wondering why."

"Why what?"

"Why everything. Why now? Why the pilgrimage, why the signature, why the pledge? What does she want from me? Why should I give her anything? Why, why, why? But no matter how I turn the subject around in my head, I have no answer. No *good* answer."

Rahz's questions burn an inferno in my brain. The calm I'd sunk into fades with talk of fighting.

He continues, "What if she is shoring up support for a war? I will *not* support that. Would my name be on a registry so I could be summoned to fight her battles? And if I refuse? Is that also treason?"

"Bu...but you can't," I stutter, alarmed. "Fight. You can't. You might get hurt."

"I'm much more worried I'd hurt someone else."

If Rahz's heart isn't the purest of them all, I'll eat raw nillyslugs for breakfast. "There won't be a war."

His gaze hardens enough to make me flinch. "You don't know that."

He's right—I don't—but I can will it with every fiber of my being. "If there's a war, you mustn't go." A thought occurs to me, and I splutter it out artlessly. "We will flee. We'll go north. On and on until the Gatekeeper's frozen palace if we must. Anything to escape war."

He arches his brows. "You would flee one danger, only to run straight into the maw of another?"

"Okay, perhaps that was a bad idea." I lock onto another dumb idea. "We'll build a boat, then. Sail across the seas."

"Jin, not all troubles are avoidable. We cannot know the future. But if I go to Lemossin, I can at least learn more of the present."

Back to that. "Don't leave me."

"I'm not leaving you. Only taking a trip to return to you with more information than we have now. The sooner I go, the sooner I'll get back."

"Soon?" My breath catches in my throat. "But Queen Aurielle gave the mixlings four months."

"One of which has nearly passed. And I'm less likely to be noticed if I go during the biggest wave, not on either end of it."

I want to yell, "I'll go with you," but I know it isn't possible. Father won't allow it. And I haven't thought things through. I can't leave, not with Mother still sleeping. She could awaken at any moment, and I must be here to greet her. I can't flee north, nor build a boat, nor accompany Rahz to Lemossin, even if we could scrounge up the money.

I press my face into Rahz's chest. He's warmed up from being under the covers with me. His heartbeat under my cheek soothes me. "This is terrible."

"Maybe it isn't." He rubs my back in little circles, chasing the worry away. Trying to. "We don't know yet."

I'm afraid to ask my next question but force the words out anyway. "When will you depart?"

"Falen must speak with Bird. She'd like to use the extra time to raise the coin needed to tag along with us, but Falen would rather get it over with. I agree. If he can get Bird to make peace with staying behind, we'll leave next week."

My muscles tense. *Next week.* My heart thuds faster. I curl my fingers in his soft sleep shirt and tug him closer. "So soon?"

Rahz kisses my forehead. "Yes, and all the sooner shall I return. Hopefully, armed with the answers to at least some of my questions."

"And...will you sign?" I already suspect he won't pledge, but maybe he'll sign? I squint my eyes shut, but I can't escape the feeling of him shaking his head.

"I'm not planning to. I don't think it's wise. As long as I make the trip, no one in the village will have any reason to suspect I didn't complete the mission."

"Falen will know."

"He seems reasonable. I have two weeks to either sway him to my point of view or, failing that, convince him my actions are my own and not to say anything to the others. I don't think he'd come running back to Vander to tattle anyway. He's above such petty acts."

I certainly hope so. Grinding my teeth, I think of Vander. I'd love to blame him for this, but it's not like he has any control over the queen's commands.

If it's anyone's fault, it's hers. She is taking my Rahz from me. Why then should I be faithful to her?

Perhaps I shouldn't. Perhaps Rahz is right after all. He often is.

"It's only a month, Jin. It'll go by before we know it."

I choke back a sob. I don't want to be sad anymore, not when I can be angry instead. Curse Aurielle for demanding this of us. We're doing fine without her, here, on our own, in Jodpirn. Why do we need the fae court anyway? What have they done for us?

Rahz weasels his big thigh between my legs and presses

against my groin. It feels nice, though my body is soft, and my mind isn't thinking of bed play. Instead, it's whirling with change.

"Let me take your mind off it, hmm?" says Rahz, his voice all low and rumbly.

Normally, that's all it would take to put me in the mood, but I feel as if I've fallen off a horse, then gotten trampled by the rest of the herd. Even sex can't fix that.

Rahz glides a hand down my back, cups my ass, and gives it a good squeeze.

I conduct my own investigation with my thigh, only to discover he isn't hard either. I'm relieved. "Maybe in the morning? For now, I just want you to hold me."

"You sure?" His arms tighten around my waist.

I nod and tuck myself as close to him as possible.

One week and this bed will be so empty without him.

One week.

Chapter Eleven

~ONE WEEK LATER~

RAHZ

AS WE EMERGE OUT OF THE SHADY PINE FOREST WE'VE traversed all morning, the view opens to a wide cloudless lavender sky and a horizon so distant as to remind me of my insignificance. The world is a huge place, and I'm just a little speck astride the slightly bigger speck called Magna.

Lemossin is approximately a twelve days' ride in this direction, assuming the horses stay healthy and the weather holds out. It would be faster if we pushed, but I could never do that to my best girl, and I get the sense Falen wouldn't do that to his horse either.

Part of me, a tiny part, is excited about the journey. I can't help it. Weeks of discovering what's around the next bend, with my only responsibilities being to take care of Magna, Falen, and myself. No neighbors asking for favors, no roofs to be shingled, no stalls to be mucked out, and no Vander to get on my last nerve.

But...

No Jindal either.

My good mood is dashed a bit every time that thought circles around. I miss him already, and it's only been half a day. Saying good-bye was one of the hardest things I've ever done.

Early this morning, he woke me before the sun with his soft lips on my neck, kissing a line just below my ear to my collarbone. And then kissing much lower. A pleasant way to wake up, indeed, but tinged with sadness as we both knew it would be our last time for quite a while.

Worry danced in his big orange eyes as he clutched my hands for the last time. "Be safe. No matter what. Take good care of yourself, and come home to me as quick as you can."

I squeezed his hands and brought them to my chest. "Promise."

We kissed good-bye then Jindal was left to stand with Bird while Falen and I mounted up and rode off.

I must have looked over my shoulder a hundred times before he disappeared into the distance.

My anger only grows. Anger at the queen, at her entire royal court, at all her advisors and their selfish demands on my time. On my very name. But I push the intrusive feeling aside. It's a beautiful day. Falen is a friendly companion and a man I'm looking forward to getting to know. I won't waste this journey on negative thoughts when there's as much to be enjoyed as there is to be upset about.

Falen rides ahead of me, sitting upon his chestnut gelding, aptly named Chestnut. He and Magna seem to get on well, so that's good, as they'll be in each other's company for the better part of the month.

Since the roadway is now wide enough to ride abreast, I urge Magna ahead until Falen and I are side by side.

"Nice view, isn't it?" The land stretches out before us, an endless sea of greens, purples, blues, and oranges, all woven like a tapestry across the rolling hills and flat fields between them.

We take in the sight, both of us slack-jawed in awe of nature's beauty. A variety of flowers grow as tall as a man with blooms wide as Samuin pumpkins. Their sweet fragrance travels on the breeze.

"It sure is. I've been this way before, but it never gets old."

I point to a patch of the giant flowers and the circle of shade beneath them. "Shall we stop for lunch?"

"In a bit, if you can wait. There's a farm up ahead with a trough for traveling horses. We can stop there."

I nod, and we grow silent as Magna and Chestnut amble downhill toward the farm. Jindal packed a huge saddlebag of food for us, courtesy of Bessa, and my stomach is rumbling just thinking about what's inside.

It takes no more than a half hour to reach the little farm-stead. True to Falen's word, the place provides water for the horses and a shady place to rest and graze a bit while we eat. I dismount and look around.

A young man comes out to check on us. Human, his brown hair shorn rather short. A smattering of freckles crosses his nose and cheeks. His grin is a friendly one. We chat with him about the weather. Then he nods in the direction of the royal capital. "You two headed for Lemossin?"

"How did you know?" asks Falen, smiling.

"Two mixlings traveling in that direction." He gestures toward the southern horizon. "Must be about that wicked pledge."

Suspicion curdles in my gut, and I knit my brows. "Wicked?"

If I'm feeling suspicious, then by the look on his face, Falen is doubly so.

"Aye." The farmer shrugs. "Asking rural folk to travel sunstrides across the country in the middle of planting season? All to sign some silly piece of parchment? It sounds right wicked if you ask me. What about the crops?"

I don't disagree, but at the same time, a sigh of relief escapes my lips. For a moment, I thought maybe he knew something I didn't. Something worse or sinister. Something truly wicked.

"Have there been many of us so far?" asks Falen. "Headed south?"

"Not too many, I reckon. A few. Definitely more than usual for this time of year, for sure."

I gather the saddlebag of Bessa's treats from Magna's back and nod toward the little wooden table nearby. "Join us for lunch? It's the least we can do to thank you for your hospitality."

"Thanks, but no thanks. Farm's not mine, and I have to get back to work. Safe travels to you both. Perhaps I'll see you in a few weeks on your way back."

"Until then." I should have known he's a worker and not an owner, since he's human. But it's not as if a human family couldn't work their own farm. Just more rare.

Falen and I settle across from each other. I unwrap the soft blue cotton cloth covering about a dozen purple longberry muffins. My mouth waters. I offer one to Falen, and his constant grin turns even cheerier.

"From Bessa?"

"There's no other."

We dig in. After the muffins, we devour cheese and dried meats, with watered dandyrose ale to wash it all down with. As usual, Bessa has thought of everything.

"We don't deserve her," says Falen.

"We really don't." I have little spare money, but my wish is to find a souvenir for her from Lemossin. Something she'd like and can't get in the smaller villages where we live. Something for Jindal as well.

To keep our costs low, we mostly plan to camp, but I've brought enough coin for a couple of nights at an inn if we need them. But the less I spend on the journey, the more I'll have for gifts. Plus, I like camping. It's fun. Nothing like the stars overhead to send a man sweet dreams.

Once the farmer is out of earshot, Falen nods in the direction he headed. "He doesn't seem to think too highly of the royal court, does he?"

Now is a bad time to mention I don't think too highly of them either. "He's probably lived his whole life farming." I shrug as if this explanation is all I have to say on the matter, when really, I've been curious how deeply Falen's trust in the court runs. "Why should he?"

Falen doesn't answer right away, which I interpret as a good sign. A thinking man can be swayed. "The court might not mean much to him now, but if something bad happened, too little rain, too much rain, if the crops failed, well, then he'd need them. I'd bet my best dagger he'd take his share of the stored grain rather than go hungry."

I concede the point for now, and we finish our lunch in companionable quiet.

With the afternoon sun warming our shoulders, we wave good-bye to the young farmer and return to the road. The horses should be good for a few hours with the weather so nice and the terrain ahead so gently sloped. We ought to make good time until sunset.

Long stretches go by with no houses or farms at all. Musk cattle graze by the dozens in herds roaming free along the countryside. Not much to do but let my mind wander and take in the peaceful scenery. If only Jinny were by my side to enjoy it, then today would be perfect.

Hopefully, he's not too sad and has found something to

keep himself busy, to keep his mind off my departure. I'm sure he'll settle back into a routine without me. Then the time will pass quickly for him. Perhaps he and Bird can get to know one another better. They've always been friendly but never close, and she's an interesting person. Her family makes clothes, all kinds. Working clothes, casual clothes, fancy dresses, frocks, and formal wear like coats, cloaks, tights, breeches, tunics. You name it, and someone in her family specializes in making it.

Maybe when I come back, Jindal will have won himself a new wardrobe somehow, full of their lovely wares. I can picture him now, preening in a new, colorful frock, teasing me to take it off him and leave him bare.

I squirm in my saddle. Magna's ears twitch back, and she huffs a snort. Point taken. That train of thought will lead to nowhere good while I'm stuck on horseback with no means of taking care of unwanted arousal. Instead, I turn my thoughts to Falen. What could I say to begin a conversation about what might happen when we reach our destination?

I need to feel him out. How open is he to the idea we don't sign after all? That we make no pledge? Perhaps we could do some digging for information on what's happening in Irondale instead. What are the queen's plans for handling the uprising? What are her thoughts on mixlings?

What does she expect of us?

Does Falen share any of my doubts? As much as I want to know, I'm hesitant to ask so soon. I wish he'd bring it up instead of me, but he seems happy to be out for a ride. Not that I'm not. It's been a lovely day. But my mind won't rest.

As the hours go by, I fear my body won't either. I'm fidgety in the saddle, and when we finally stop to make camp for the night at the edge of a grove of old poplar trees, I'm restless.

Instead of using my magic for a fire, I set about gathering wood because I need something to do. Falen takes care of the horses.

We eat. We chat about nothing of importance. We spread out our bedrolls and prepare for sleep.

Without Jindal at my side, I know I won't sleep well. But it's been a long day, and though I'm still feeling unsettled, exhaustion creeps in on the moonlight's silver tendrils and carries me under.

Chapter Twelve

Jindal

I'M GRUMPY, AND MY BODY HURTS.

I haven't had a good night's rest since Rahz left, and I feel the effects in the tension of my muscles, the headache throbbing low in my skull, and the inflammation around my joints. It's easy to forget how important sleep is to your health until you've had seven long nights without it. Tossing and turning, reaching for an absent lover, is the stuff of nightmares.

I keep thinking I'll get used to this. I'm the lucky one, still sleeping in our bed. The sheets still smell like us, and if I stuff my face into Rahz's pillow, the lingering scent of his hair brings me comfort. But not sleep. Poor Rahz. He's out in the middle of nowhere, sleeping on a pad on the ground, without knowing what the next day will bring. Knowing it's worse for him only makes me more upset.

Ugh. And if I have to listen to Vander complain about "the humans this" or "the humans that" one more time, I'm going to cram a nillyslug so far down his throat he'll choke on it.

Today has been another long day in a string of long days. Rahz's absence makes my father's presence even more grating than usual. I hadn't realized how much Rahz served as a buffer between us until he was gone and I was left to handle the old man myself. He's ornery, unreasonable, and getting on my last nerve.

Sometimes I wonder what Mother ever saw in him. One day, after she's awoken and we've gotten to know each other, perhaps I'll ask. I like to think her waking will cheer him up. That suddenly he'll become jovial. Appreciative. That maybe he'll even love me.

But this line of thought is pointless. Mother is dormant. Rahz is gone. I'm exhausted, and the only thing I can do to get my mind off my woes is head to The Golden Wing, our local tavern. I'll drink some ale and take pleasure in the company of our friends.

Hopefully, Vander isn't there.

Vander is there.

After I shove open the heavy wooden door, he's the first thing I see, seated at the bar, drink in hand, mouth spewing some story no one seems to be paying much attention to.

Curses. Just my luck.

My bad mood dips lower. Oh well, I'm here now, and I won't leave because he's here too. But still, can't one thing go right? One thing?

Luckily, Bird is at the other end of the bar, so I make my way over to her.

The inside of The Golden Wing is warmly lit with a combination of flickering oil lamps and magically charmed lights, which glow golden and flutter around the thick wooden rafters in pairs of tiny, perfectly shaped wings, hence the name. A dozen tables are scattered throughout, booths line the far wall, and a large hearth frames a cold fireplace, not currently in use. Colorful tapestries, woven locally, mostly by Lemon and Salah's family, adorn the walls. Beautiful landscapes, bountiful farms, frolicking unicorns, and fields of flowers lend a whimsical feeling to the place.

I slide onto the stool next to Bird. "Good evening."

"Oh, hello, Jinny." Her smile looks a bit like my own. Faked. So she's not happy either. Not that I blame her. She and Falen only met a year or so ago. To be separated so early in their courtship must be a heavy yoke to bear. "What brings you around tonight?"

"Same as you, I imagine." I catch the barkeep's gaze and signal her over. "I'm lonely without Rahz around."

She huffs a breath out her nose. "And it's only been a week. We have at least three more to go."

"Don't remind me." Time passes slow as snails without Rahz to keep me company. "They must be at least halfway to Lemossin by now."

"At least." She takes a sip of something pink and fruity looking.

Emorine, the barkeep, approaches. Her expression says, back again? but in a friendly way. I don't usually show up at The Golden Wing this frequently. "What can I get you?"

"I'll have whatever Bird is having. It smells like frosted fruit cake." I lick my lips. "And I'll buy a second for her as well, since she's almost done."

Emorine's chuckle brings a grin to my lips. It's nice to feel a real smile on my face. "You'll love it. Tastes just like a frosted fruit cake too."

"What's it called?"

"Lollyberries and cream."

"It's paradise in a cup," says Bird with a little hiccup.

"I'll remember that for next time."

"Don't drink too many, though. They have a way of sneaking up on you." Emorine's tall white wings flutter on her back as if to emphasize the warning. She heads off to make the drinks.

Bird beams, revealing matching dimples on each plump cheek. "Thanks for the drink, Jin."

"My pleasure."

Vander's voice cuts loudly through our conversation. "What would you know about the south? You've never even been there."

We both cringe and ignore him. I don't know the fae he's talking to, and if they're friends of his, I probably don't want to know them either.

"So." Bird steers my attention back toward her. "What are you doing to keep busy?"

"Um, nothing? Chores, as usual. Work on the farm. In my spare time, I mope and wallow. You?"

She tuts. "Don't mope and wallow. It's unbecoming. If I were you, I'd spend my free time with Bessa learning how to cook so her pastry recipes don't go to the grave with her someday."

I blink and close my mouth. My chest tightens, and I sink a bit farther in my seat, shoulders drooped. Bird is speaking casually, her tone light, but bringing up Bessa's mortality so blithely doesn't sit well with me. Bessa isn't old. Well, she's not very old, only fortysome cycles, and humans can live to be a hundred, so she has many left. Her inevitable death isn't something I've given much thought to. But now I have yet another reason to be sad.

"Oh, Jinny. I'm sorry, I shouldn't have said that. I only meant you might enjoy spending more time with her."

My face must have given me away. "It's okay. It's a good suggestion. I try not to be underfoot when she's working, but maybe if I offered to help, she wouldn't mind."

"Of course she wouldn't mind. She loves you dearly."

She does. Aside from Rahz, she's probably the only one who does. I'd like to believe somewhere under his gruff exterior, my father loves me, but I really can't be sure. He makes it hard to tell.

Emorine returns with our drinks. "Cheers."

We echo out thank-yous, and I take my first swallow. Crisp and creamy on my tongue, the tartness of the lollyberries and the sweetness of honeyed syrup blend into a perfect concoction of alcoholic divinity. I groan. "You weren't kidding when you said paradise in a cup!"

Bird laughs and sips at her own glass. "You're welcome."

"I could drink ten of these."

"Please don't. The last thing I want to do is carry you home tonight and explain to your father I got you drunk off berries and cream."

"Yeah, I don't want that either." I can imagine it now, the look in his eyes, the disapproval. No, thank you. We're clinking glasses when Vander's shouting overtakes us.

"—fine without 'em!" He must be drunk. He's annoying, but usually, he doesn't bellow this loudly. "Don't need all that magic anyway."

I turn my head and narrow my gaze.

"A hard day's work is good for us." Vander lifts his chin. His audience murmurs their agreement. "We don't need 'em."

Surely, he's not talking about—

"Falen has no extra magic, and Rahz only uses his so we'll feel like we owe him something. But we don't. Nobody does. He's lucky we—" Vander won't get to finish that sentence.

Because I see red. My cheeks burn. I'm up from my seat and in his face before the thought has materialized. "You dare speak of my mate while he's not here to defend himself? Coward!"

Vander's pupils have near swallowed his irises. How many drinks has he had? His glare is hard, and spittle flies as he talks. "What, so you think you're going to stand up for him? You? Little Jinny? I'd like to see you try."

Vander is bigger than me. And stronger. But he's drunk, and

I'm not. He also isn't defending the honor of the love of his life, and I am.

I punch him square in the jaw. "That's for Rahz."

I rear back and do it again. "And that's for me."

The look on his face says he wasn't expecting the first punch. Or the second. Before he can react, I flutter out of his reach and shake out my hand. My knuckles hurt. I've never hit someone before. Did I break something? Are my bones okay?

His face turns purple with anger. The fae around him are laughing, hiding grins behind their hands, and backing away. Even his friends seem to be enjoying Vander brought down a peg.

"How dare you?" He shoots up, but two sets of hands grab his arms and haul him back down.

"I think you'll find I had every right." I huff my indignation. "Hold your tongue and cease insulting the one I love, and maybe I won't hit you again." I'd stomp my foot for emphasis, but I'm in the air, so I can't. Best not land just yet. I'm more agile than Vander this way, should his friends let him go.

But they don't. Vander rubs his jaw and glares daggers at me but doesn't try to leave his spot at the bar again.

Bird is at my side. "I can't believe you hit him."

"You finished?" asks Emorine from below, her snowy white brows arched to amused crescents. "I'd say no fighting in my bar, but he deserved it well enough."

Vander scowls at her.

She shrugs it off and beckons me. "Come down and finish your drink and leave him to sulk it off."

I do just that, my chest puffed in pride. Not that hitting people is generally something to be proud of, but standing up for Rahz is.

And I will always stand up for Rahz.

Chapter Thirteen

Rahz

We're one river crossing away from Lemossin, and I'm still no closer to discovering if Falen's loyalty to Queen Aurielle will override his loyalty to a friend. To me. Because we have become friends, Falen and I, in these two weeks of riding long days, pitching tents on cool, rainy nights, and talking about anything and everything except for the most pressing matter.

If he signs this pledge and I don't, will he report me for treason?

I gaze past him toward the mighty Onyx River that bisects Luminia. Never in my life did I think I'd see its ebony waters with my own eyes. Hard to believe a river so wide even exists, much less that the fae have engineered a ferry system to get people, horses, and wagons across it.

"Almost there now." Falen stares into the distance, same as me.

"To think we'll be sleeping in the capital city tonight." My chest is tight as nerves and excitement take turns coursing through my body. I've never seen such a sight.

Lemossin is huge. Past the river and uphill, the beginning of the city sprawls impossibly big. Even from this distance, I make out a great gate with towering walls on either side, winding streets farther uphill beyond the wall, and rows and rows of buildings split by vast greenlands inside the city. And Falen says the part we can see from the river crossing is only a fraction of the city, most of which spills down the other side of the mount.

Fifty of our little Jodpirns could easily fit into the visible portion alone.

We approach the river alongside other travelers. Merchants with wagonloads of wares in tow, mixlings on horseback, a band of performers, maybe acrobats, with colorful props and the sort of wagon that can be lived in, and even a few noblemen clad in luxurious velvets despite the midday warmth.

I'm curious about them all. I'd love to poke my head into that bright red wagon. Would they have a tiny little house built inside? What must that life be like?

At the ramp, those with wings simply take flight, leaving the working crew to handle their horses and belongings. Falen's wings are nearly as large as a full fae's, but they're flightless. Could he glide if the wind currents were just right? That would be a dangerous theory to prove, though.

When it's our turn to board the sturdy-looking ferry, we dismount and lead Magna and Chestnut on foot.

"Why don't you go first?" I gesture for Falen to pass us.

Magna has never set hoof on a ferry, doesn't particularly care for water, and is often shy of new experiences. Luckily, Chestnut is a stalwart traveler and takes to the ferry with ease. His calm, easy-going manner, along with my gentle coaxing, is enough to convince Magna to board without any fuss, though her eyes are wide and her ears are pinned back. She gives a nervous head toss and throws me a look that says, "See the things I do for you?"

I rub her neck and promise her extra apples if she's good. To be honest, I'm as nervous as she is. I've never been on a boat of any sort, and though this one seems safe, the boards beneath my feet move with the river in a way that tricks my balance and flips my stomach.

"You can ride with them if you like." A sailor points out the rail along the stalls. "Or take seats up front."

As much as I'd like to see the view from the front, I know Magna needs me. "I'll stay with her, thanks."

"Me too." Falen urges Chestnut into a slot large enough for one horse and one man.

I settle Magna into the next one. Side by side, all four of us have a view of upstream, the eastern flank of the river, and that's nearly as good as being at the front.

"We'll set off in ten." The sailor passes us, directing the next set of travelers.

Nobody has asked a fee for passage. Anyone can board the ferry and cross the river at their leisure. It travels back and forth all day, every day, barring bad weather. Thankfully, I don't have to part with any of my coin for this adventure. A free boat ride is infinitely better than a paid one.

Falen climbs the rail between our stalls, thighs on the higher plank, feet tucked beneath the lower one to hold himself in place. Looks comfortable, but I'd better stand on my own two feet if the swaying of the ferry is anything to go by, or else I might be sick.

Falen grins. "Your stomach all right?"

"Uh. You can tell just by looking?"

"Don't worry. It's a short ride once we're off. Here." He turns, rustles in one of his saddlebags, grabs a hunk of bread, and hands it over. "Might actually be better if you eat something. I hear motion sickness is worse on an empty stomach."

"Thanks. It's not too bad." *Yet.* I bite off a hunk of the bread just in case. Better to be on the safe side.

Aside from the horses—ours and about a dozen other animals, unattended because they must be accustomed to this crossing—we're alone. The ferry is quite large, and the river noisy enough to drown out conversation.

This is as good a time as any. "Hey, Falen. I've been meaning to ask you something."

His nut-brown eyes focus on mine in that friendly way he has. "Sure."

A deep breath helps to settle my nerves. Whether the answer is good or bad, I need to know before we enter those gates. "What would you think if I..." I chicken out for a moment, staring at the bread instead of him. "If I didn't sign the queen's registry after all?"

Confusion twists his features. "But we came all this way?" He doesn't look offended, just curious. That's a good sign.

Probably.

"Yes, well, I had to do that, didn't I? Or Vander would never have let it rest. But what he doesn't know won't hurt him." Or me, if I'm lucky.

"You don't want to be on the registry?" His voice has gone low. So quiet as to be sure our conversation remains private.

I shake my head and keep my voice down too. "We don't know what it's for."

"You don't trust their motives."

"I don't." If my stomach was churning before, it's practically flailing now, and not because of the river. Falen's considering gaze, the intelligence in his bright eyes, and the slight downward turn of his lips have me on edge. I want to keep him as a friend, but I want my business to remain my own even more.

"What do you think will happen?" he asks.

The open-ended question stumps me. "You mean if I sign?"

"That, and in general. The fighting in the south. The registry. The pledge. It must be connected, all happening at once like this. What's she preparing for, and how do we fit in?"

The fact that he asks these questions gives me some measure of relief. I've been asking myself the same things ad nauseam. "I don't know, but my gut says it isn't good. I'm afraid to be called to fight and to be put into a position where refusal isn't an option."

Falen presses his lips to a thin line and tips his head. "The thought has crossed my mind as well."

"But you like her, don't you?"

"The queen? Yes, but as a child likes a hero in a storybook, so to speak. I realize my limited experience doesn't count for much. I don't know Aurielle or Lord Waren. Not really. Though I have briefly met the princess, Suvi, and found her to be as charming as you'd expect. It's hard to believe they'd mean us any harm. My gut says they mean well."

The dinging of a shrill bell startles me and Magna both. I stroke her neck as a booming voice calls, "All aboard."

"We'll be off soon, then." Falen shifts to a more secure position, effectively ending our conversation before I've received the reassurance I'm looking for. "May want to hang on to the rail."

I do that. One hand calming Magna, the other white-knuckled around the rail as the ferry lurches into motion. "Wow." It's almost as if I can feel the water beneath my feet.

Falen smiles. "It's rather fascinating, isn't it? A ship this large traversing the river?"

"How is it propelled?"

Falen points to the ropes overhead. "It's a combination of methods, depending on conditions. A rope and cable system that spans the river, oars that can be churned by either muscle or magic, sails when the wind is right. A modern marvel."

"Indeed." A sudden longing so fierce my heart pounds rises within me. If only Jindal were here to see this. He'd love it. The water. The ingenuity. The adventure.

Well, maybe not the adventure so much. Jindal is a bit of a

homebody. But if I could paint a picture of this view to send to him so he could witness the beauty along with me, I would.

Falen has a faraway expression on his face. I get the feeling he might be thinking along the same lines about Bird.

As much as I like Falen, it's a shame we're here with each other instead of with our mates. How romantic would it be to kiss in the middle of the largest river in the world?

"Rahz." Falen's attention is on me now, intense, but not unwelcome. "I will tell no one if you decide not to sign. Or not to pledge. It isn't anyone's business but your own."

A weight falls from my shoulders, and the pleasant warmth of true friendship fills my chest. "Thank you, Falen. And should you change your mind about things, you can expect the same from me."

He thrusts a hand forward, and we clasp wrists. His skin glimmers like that of the fae, while mine is sun-ruddy like a human's, but his shake is firm and full of trust.

If only every disagreement were so easily handled.

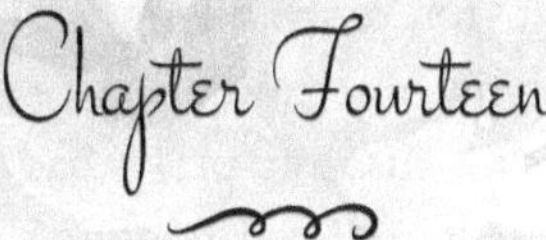

Chapter Fourteen

Jindal

"You?" Bessa glares at me from the other side of her kitchen table, hands on her waist, brows arched in such a disbelieving fashion that should be insulting, but only makes me laugh. "Want to learn to cook? After all these years?"

It's not that I want to learn to cook exactly—though that will be a pretty useful side-effect—it's more that Bessa has been on my mind lately. Though she's been like family to me my whole life, I don't know her as well as I should. I know her heart, her generosity, her kindness, which she gives to me so freely. But who is Bessa, really? What does she like? How does she feel? What does she long for in life?

Once Bird gave me the idea to ask for cooking lessons, I couldn't let it go. It's the perfect ruse for all my questions.

"Are you trying to put me out of a job, youngling?" she sasses, her tone light, but it only reminds me that this is her work. We're not her real family.

"Never." I cross my heart with my fingers. "I'm lonely

without Rahz, and I don't wish to be underfoot, so I thought if I learned to help, maybe you'd let me hang around?"

Her expression softens like the petals of a morning flower unfurling. "Of course you can hang around. You don't need to learn to cook for that. You're always my favorite company."

Her words touch my heart and bring a smile to my lips.

She pats my cheek. "Miss him pretty bad, don't you?"

"So bad." Like half my soul is gone, leaving me with an empty place inside that only Rahz's return can fill. I hope he and Falen are well, and they're on their way back, but it's probably too soon for that. Ugh. We're not even halfway through our separation, and I'm already losing my mind without him.

Bessa gestures to the kitchen stools. "Pull up a chair. I'll be baking bread this afternoon. You may as well learn how to make the dough."

We're at her house, not mine. She rents a little cottage in town, just two rooms, but more than enough for one person. The delicious aroma of freshly baked bread lingers, even though there isn't any yet. The scent must have permeated the very walls. I love it so much I suck in a deep breath through my nose and savor it.

I've been here before, but since she's at my place so often, this is an unusual setting for us. Arguably, Father's kitchen is her territory, but her own is even more so. Evidence of Bessa's care surrounds us. Handmade yellow curtains with green ivy embroidery frame each window, the little clay figurine of a sheep I sculpted for her when I was small stands guard over a petite bookshelf brimming with tomes, and a pile of abandoned knitting waits in her favorite chair. The atmosphere is cozy. I like being at Bessa's place.

I grab a stool and pull it up to the long wooden counter. Bessa has already coated the surface in flour.

"Most bread recipes need a leaven." Bessa holds a glass jar out for my inspection. Inside is a white, bubbly, sour-smelling substance. I've seen her use this before. "It'll make the loaf rise. Without it, you get a lump of brick. Edible but not ideal. We want our bread fluffy."

"Start with leaven. Got it."

"No, you start with your dry ingredients. Flour, salt, maybe a little sugar if you're feeling frisky." She dumps these into a mixing bowl and digs a little trench at the center. "The leaven and water go here, and we mix until the dough comes together. If it's too wet or sticky, add more flour. Too dry or crumbly, add more water."

"Makes sense." I watch her work as I've done many times before. Bessa's strong, capable hands scoop and mix in a quick, practiced motion. "I know what comes next."

She arches a singular brow. "Do you now?"

"Yes. We knead the dough. Over and over for an eternity." Or at least it felt that way when I was a child.

Bessa chuckles. "More like twenty minutes, but yes. That's next. You can help with that part while I mix a second batch."

"Who is the next batch for?"

"Both of these will go to the beekeeper. I'm trading them for the honeycomb I use in my pastries."

I grin. "A very worthy cause indeed."

When she smiles, her cheeks plump, and her eyes crinkle at the corners. Age lines have formed there like they do in all humans eventually. They'll only deepen with time, and though they're beautiful, it makes me sad to think of Bessa getting older.

"What's your favorite recipe?" I ask. It's as good a place to start as any.

A thoughtful expression sweeps her features. "My favorite? Hmm, I don't know. We both know Rahz's favorite is my apricot pastries, and I know your favorite is my cheesy potatoes. But my favorite? Let me think."

She mixes the dough idly while her gaze drifts upward.

Without her noticing, I memorize her every feature, locking this moment into my mind forever as a day I will treasure.

After a time, she says, "My mulberry pudding is rather nice, isn't it?"

"Delicious." A good thing I ate before I came, or this conversation would surely make me hungry.

"That's my favorite, then. Mulberry pudding."

I resolve to remember this for later, when the mulberries ripen in a few months. I'll trade some of our early bean crop for them and bring Bessa a whole bucketful. She'll be able to make all the pudding her heart desires.

And knowing Bessa, she'll share.

"Here you are." She plops the dough in front of me. "Remember how?"

"Yes." I get to work kneading and folding the dough while Bessa begins the second batch. "How do I tell when it's done?"

"The texture changes. It's rough and a little bit sticky now, but as you work the dough, it'll get stretchier. Smoother. You can test it by pressing a patch with your fingers. It should spring back slowly, leaving only a small indent. I'll show you."

We work in companionable silence as I ponder how to phrase my next question. Will she think it's weird for me to be asking about her personal life? Will she answer?

"Bessa?" I let her name float between us, unable to go on without her invitation.

"Yes, love?"

"Did you ever want children of your own?"

Well, it's out of me. No clawing it back in.

Her ever-moving hands come to a stop inside the bowl. I know better than to quit kneading, so I go on as if this question were more casual than it is.

She's watching me, but I can't bring myself to look away from the dough.

"Why do you ask?"

I shrug and readjust my wings, a nervous habit. "Just curious. There's so much I don't know about you."

Slowly her hands return to motion. "I've thought about having children, but never seriously. For one, who would be their father?" This last part she says with a hint of laughter in her voice, which brings me straight to my next question.

"Do you have a beau? I've never met your beau."

"If I wasn't covered in flour, I'd swat you for that. You know I don't have a beau, silly. Do you think I could hide an entire extra person from you?" She shakes her head as if I'm being ridiculous. "When you were young, I could barely sneak off to the bathroom by myself, much less hide a beau. At least you don't follow me around like a little duckling anymore."

She doesn't mean for me to feel bad. Of course she doesn't. But I do anyway. "Is it my fault you don't have kids?"

She turns, brows creasing. "Is that what this is about, Jinny?" She brings her hands out of the bowl, flour and all, and grabs my shoulders. "What's happening in that pretty head of yours?"

"You're human. You don't have forever like... I want you to have everything you want."

"I don't want more kids." She squeezes my shoulders for emphasis. "I have you. I *want* you."

Her effort to reassure me is appreciated, but I can't let it go yet. "But you thought about it?"

"Impossible not to. It's just something people think about." She lifts her shoulders a little. "But even if I did want more children, which I don't, that wouldn't affect my love for you. And you'd have a very important job."

"What's that?" My voice sounds small, even to my ears.

"Big brother." She lets me go. "Of course."

My chest is all warm, and I don't know what to do with myself. Thankfully, there's still dough to knead, so I do that.

"What's got you asking these questions?" She goes back to her mixing as well, which makes it a little easier for me to talk.

"I've had a lot to think about lately with the way things are. And the changes. Can I ask you another question?"

"Anything you like."

"Do you ever wish you were born fae and not human?"

She frowns into her mixing bowl. "That's complicated."

Boy, do I know. "I just wondered."

"Does Rahz have something to do with this?"

Yes. Rahz has something to do with everything. "Not only Rahz."

Bessa takes her time answering. A deep breath in and out, a few passes of her hands over the dough, countless tittering heartbeats in my chest.

"It's hard not to want what you don't have in life. Would I like the respect of others to come naturally? Easily? Yes. Would I like my own land? Yes. Would I like to fly among the clouds as you do?" She flicks flour onto my wings and winks. "Absolutely, yes. But do I like being human? I do. I like my big, strong body and my sense of time. My identity. If I could trade, I'm not sure I would. You see how it's complicated?"

I nod, taking everything in, turning each thought in my mind, trying to make sense of her position. "You don't feel as though you are respected?"

"Not in the same way you are, youngling. Surely you see that much."

I don't. Or I hadn't. But I'm beginning to. And if Bessa feels this way, then it must be true. But it's all so unfair.

"Have you and Rahz spoken about this?" she asks. "How does he feel?"

"Some yes, though I'm coming to think he's been protecting me from the worst of it."

"He's a sweet boy. You're lucky to have each other."

This I can agree with wholeheartedly. "I'm the lucky one."

"Him too. You're also a sweet boy. Clever, funny, loving. You have many a charm, my love, and you're growing more compassionate with each passing season. I'm proud of you."

A surge of joy so strong it brings tears to my eyes zings through me. "Oh, Bessa."

"Don't cry in my dough, Jin," she warns, a teasing hint to her tone. "Otherwise, we'll have no honey for the apricot pastries I plan to make to welcome Rahz and Falen home with."

"You are the best, Bessa. *The best.* I love you so."

"And I you." She smacks my hands, which have gone still in the dough. "Now back to work."

So grateful I could burst, I do as I'm told.

And I continue to think. To wrap my mind around new thoughts and hold it open for whatever is to come. Because it feels like something is coming. And I plan to be ready.

Chapter Fifteen

Rahz

FOR TWO NIGHTS AND ONE DAY, I'VE BEEN HAUNTING the streets of Lemossin, scouring every nook and cranny for useful information. The city is like a whole different world than back home in Jodpirn. Here, folks speak openly about the conflict, the brewing escalation, the threat of war.

They say with no artifice that the southern lands are in turmoil, the humans are revolting—they're coming out of hiding to loot and riot until they're slain or chased away by a makeshift fae militia—the trade routes are compromised, the mixlings must prove their loyalty, and the queen prepares to act.

The humans here are skittish, going about their work with fearful expressions, twitchy movements, and one eye always on the palace guards as if they expect something. Would my mother be safe in Lemossin? The answer is no. I wouldn't want her within a ten-hour ride of the city, much less within its stifling walls.

We have no extra coin nor extra time to linger much longer.

Today we'll do what we've come to do, then turn around and head home.

Over the bustling streets, the marble behemoth called Ralossi Palace looms tall into the gray, cloudy sky. Falen and I are headed to its gilded public entrance, him to make his pledge and sign the registry, and me to sneak away and learn what else there is to learn.

The other mixlings I've seen seem to be eager for their fleeting time in the presence of royalty. Ready to embrace their fae side and leave the humans in the dust. Of course I'm only seeing the ones who made the journey. How many others are like me? Staying at home, hiding, or pretending to make this journey for the look of it. I won't see them haunting the grounds of Lemossin, will I?

Falen is less eager and more suspicious than the others, and part of me feels bad for that. My own doubts have crept into his judgment when he'd have been happy to go on putting the royal family on a pedestal, as he's done since his youth. That and what we've heard in our short time here has jaded him.

He leans in and points. "There's a group headed up the stairs. Should we join them?" Then in a lower voice, "The bigger the group, the easier for you to slip away."

"Good idea." We've already discussed our plans. Falen will act the obedient mixling, waiting in line, signing his name, pledging, while I try to find someone within the palace—someone who might know what the queen is planning—to talk to.

Guilt sits heavily in my gut at the thought of what I must do. How I must use my magic. Aside from my mother, Jindal, and now Falen, no one knows the extent of my abilities.

I'm not comfortable with mind magic. It's forbidden, and for good reason. What could be more wrong than to peer into someone's innermost thoughts, to coax their secrets from them with just a little push of my power, to force them to do my bidding? I feel dirty even considering it, but I see no other way to get to the bottom of things.

I'll be careful. So careful. I'll stay on the subject and only gather the information I need. I won't sink too deep. But someone must know what the royal family is up to.

Someone must warn the humans.

We join the group Falen indicated, smiles all around. Can they see that mine is fake? That inside, I'm trembling? My nerves run rampant through my body, but I tamp them down to find inner calm. I need my wits about me if I'm going to pull this off.

As we ascend the fancy staircase, our feet clap on the expensive stone. Cornflower blue striated lines wind through the pearlescent white of the marble, each step gleaming with well-polished shine. On either side, palace guards stand in a row, more casual than I'd have guessed, chatting with each other but still keeping an eye on things. They don't look like they're expecting a revolt anytime soon. How much of the royal plans do they know, and how much remains unspoken?

The other mixlings talk among themselves while I search for an easy spot to dart into the shadows, but nothing is dark here. The walls are white and gold, the pillars are white and gold, and even the ceilings are white and gold. Faerie lights glow crisply from overhead, lighting the interior brighter than the gloomy daylight outside.

No, sneaking will not be easy in this place.

We are herded through the enormous entryway into a grand hall bigger than any room I've ever been in. My whole house could fit into this hall four times over with room to spare. In this section, the ceiling is all but gone, as the space is enchanted to look open to the skies, but even those who couldn't sense the spell would know it to be fake. Outside, the day promises rain. Maybe a storm. Inside, sunny skies and pink, fluffy clouds looking sweet enough to eat tower over us.

Nothing here is real.

Even the ground beneath our feet is enchanted. A rippling wave of greens, purples, and blues, enough to make a person dizzy if they look down too long. I doubt my nose as the piercing scent of witch hazel wafts to my nostrils. Its flowers bloom in late fall and winter, not early spring, so why does it smell this way?

Falen takes in the interior with wide eyes, the same as me. I've never seen anything like this, such opulence, such splendor. But what I need to do now is focus, not ogle.

I sweep the room, looking for an exit. There are several. If I get caught, I'll pretend I overindulged and need the facilities, which isn't a great plan but better than no plan at all.

Or I'll use my mind magic, but only if I have to.

Catching Falen's gaze, I nod in the direction I intend to go. Subtly he returns the gesture. Then he turns to the others and points in the opposite direction.

"Have you ever seen a faerie light so bright? I haven't."

They follow his finger, and I steal my shot, parting from the group and making a beeline between pillars to an open archway along the perimeter. In a few heartbeats, I'm through it and into a long hallway beyond, blessedly not lit so shockingly bright.

With a quick spell to deaden the sound of my footsteps and cloak myself in shadow, I mask my presence as best I can. I'm not invisible, exactly, nothing like that—even I'm not that powerful —just easy to overlook.

I turn in the same direction as our group was headed, traveling parallel to the vast hall. The ceilings here are gray stone, tall, and arched. Oil lamps glow a warm orange, the color of Jindal's eyes in the twilight, and I'm the only one creeping around.

It's an odd feeling to be alone in Ralossi Palace, somewhere I never thought I'd be. Falen has told me a large court of nobles mill around Queen Aurielle wherever she goes. I'll seek out one of these folks. Someone close to the queen but not in the throne room with her. Someone on their way or perhaps just leaving.

Someone I can enchant to follow me for a quick conversation. A few fast questions.

Even if I learn nothing, it's worth a try.

Four guards pass by in sets of two, but my enchantment holds strong. I call no attention to myself, and they don't notice me. Once they're gone, I gasp for air. Holding my breath won't make me any less obvious, but it's instinct. I suck in a deep breath. Ah, that's better.

Another group crosses my path, not ten feet in front of me. Nobles or merchants, I can't tell. Their clothes are nice but not *so* nice I'd believe them to be close enough to the queen to have the information I seek. This time I practice breathing in and out, slow and steady, and they continue on their way without seeing me.

The hallway seems endless until it doesn't. I arrive at an impasse, turn right, and hope. Inside, I'm trembling, but outside, I'm slick as oil, seeping unnoticed through the cracks of perception.

Muffled voices drift toward me from farther along, and I head straight for them. No time to back down now. My magic is being tested to its limits. Maybe I should have practiced these darker skills more often, but who would have thought I'd need them?

First, I spot a set of guards and behind them a small group of nobles, perhaps even royalty. I study their finery, their jewels, their posture. I don't know enough to tell the difference between the royal family and the richest of nobles, but these people look like money. But which one should I aim for?

On silent feet, I creep closer. In the center of the group stands a young lady with shimmering purple hair. Not plum, like Jindal's, but more lavender or maybe amethyst, with a bejeweled circlet around her head boasting pure, clear quartz crystals.

She's petite, smaller than the rest of the group yet somehow standing out as the most prominent member. Perhaps it's the way the others circle her, chattering at her like she can listen to six people at once. All the while she keeps a pleasant but bland expression on her pretty oval face.

Her wings are a dusky gray-blue, the color of storm clouds, and her dress is a bold sapphire that complements them beautifully. Everyone's eyes are trained on her, but hers...are trained on me.

Uh-oh.

Panic shatters my fragile calm. How can she see me? She'll know I don't belong here. If she sounds the alarm, I'm done for. Already my spell is unraveling as her pale pink gaze breaks my concentration.

She shakes her head, a minute movement directed straight to me, then glances purposefully to her right.

I follow her gaze to a set of stairs. Empty, at least at the moment. It's clear she wants me to take them, but what's unclear is why. I'm afraid of walking straight into a trap.

Still, she could have outed me easily just now and didn't. At least not yet. And out of all the people I could have found to speak to, she is certainly the biggest jackpot. For this must be Princess Suvi, even more beautiful than Falen described. She's the right age, the right coloring, and definitely possesses the right effortless authority over the room.

I refocus on my magic, holding it together while dodging their group and making for the stairs. I can't let the question go. Is she leading me into a trap? Could be. But my gut says no.

Her attention drifts back to the others. She nods and answers their inquiries, then somehow disperses them all with a slight gesture of her tiny hand.

I'm lurking halfway up the staircase. What should I do next? She looks right at me, rolls her eyes, and arches her brows as if to say, Still there? Shoo! Up the stairs!

I scurry up the rest of the way and wait in a well-appointed antechamber full of places to sit and expensive-looking decorations to ogle. Delicate little tables with spindly legs and fancy knickknacks sit atop them, tall vases with fresh flowers inside, and colorful artwork in ornate golden frames. The casual wealth of this place is stifling.

She doesn't make me wait long—thank goodness because my nerves are on a knife's edge—and arrives with only one guard in tow, which comes as a surprise. She must not think I'm much of a threat. I mean, I'm not, or well, I don't intend to be. But I could be, I think. Unless...

Is her magic stronger than mine? That would be a first. I'm almost excited to find out when I remember I probably should be scared.

She's standing still on the threshold, watching me. I remember my manners and lurch into an awkward bow.

Her ringing laughter fills my ears. "Rise. And do tell me who you are and what you want before I call the rest of my guards back."

Her voice is as lovely as the rest of her, lilting and sweet but somehow still brooking no argument.

Nillyslugs. How does one address royalty? I should have paid more attention to this lesson in school. "Erm, milady." I deepen my bow and frantically consider my words. The urge to tell her the truth is overwhelming, so strong it can't be real. Is that her magic? If so, it's countering mine. "My name is of no importance. I'm here to learn."

I risk a glance at her face and find an amused expression. "I said rise. You're terrible at that anyway." She flutters her hand at me and my unpracticed bow.

I straighten and send my magic scouring hers. Like two opposing currents, they meet, mix, and fizzle away, only to rise again as we rush to protect ourselves.

"I'll make a deal with you." Her unwavering gaze is both shrewd and curious. "I'll hold back my magic if you hold back yours, and we'll speak like two people who *both* want to learn."

Too good to be true? I don't care. I have to risk it. "Yes, milady." With a relaxing loosening of my muscles, my mind also eases, letting the enchantments drift away.

"I'm Suvi," she begins. "And you're a mixling. The others are busy signing their names on an official registry, but you won't even tell me yours. Why?"

It's only fair she plays the first gambit. I'm in her home, invading her city, not the other way around. "I'm afraid of what it's for. What if I don't want to be called to fight?"

"You think it's a draft? To recruit soldiers for an army?"

"Isn't it? What else could it be?"

She gives a dainty shrug. "A list of those with human ancestry to be given more land?"

I arch my brows. No way am I dumb enough to buy that.

"It's a draft. If too many of you side with humans, it could turn the tides of power. Fae need mixlings on our side. That's not so secret."

"Isn't it? I'm from farther north where it's fifty-fifty whether or not the people believe the revolt in the south is happening."

This does seem to surprise her. "Really? They don't know?"

I nod. "It's easier to pretend when it's not in front of your face. It's different here. Everyone acts as if the brewing war is common knowledge."

"It is."

My stomach lurches at her simple honesty. At what those two words mean. No matter how often I hear talk of war getting batted around as if it might really happen, it's no less a punch in the gut now. But from the lips of Princess Suvi? It's like I've been hit by a battering ram.

"When?"

"Soon. Will you fight?"

My head shakes without permission from my brain. No. I won't hurt humans. I won't kill them. They're near to defenseless in this realm already, with no power, no wealth, no status to call their own. The queen is nothing more than a bully if she plans to subdue them with a fae and mixling army, and I won't be part of it.

"Not at all?" she asks carefully. "Or not for my mother?" Intelligent pink eyes stare a hard line through my soul.

This is dangerous territory. I could be killed for less. "Not for your mother."

"You'd protect the humans who rebelled against the crown?"

"I'd protect *my mother.*"

"Ah." Her expression softens. "So you don't plan to fight unless the fighting breaches the north? Why come at all, then?"

I'm getting tired of this one-sided interrogation. "Are you the only one allowed to ask questions in this conversation?"

"I don't think so, but while your tongue is tied, do you really expect me to hold back mine?"

"Why are you talking to me at all?"

She narrows her gaze as she considers me. A muscle in her jaw twitches. At length, she says, "I've been looking for an opportunity just like this among the mixlings who've come pouring through the Great Hall to pledge. When all this time I should've been looking for the ones cloaked in magic sneaking around our castle passageways."

"Why?"

"My reasons are my own, but you needn't fear me. I want peace between our species."

"And your mother doesn't?"

"She wants to maintain the status quo through any means necessary. I want peace through *peaceful* means. Neither of us is likely to get what we want." Her lips turn down at that. "And you and I must be careful while she is queen and I am not."

The wind punches from my lungs. She could be killed for saying less, for revealing those intentions at all, let alone to a common mixling. I feel as if we're on more even footing, but I won't risk telling her my name. Not when I could still run. Still hide.

"Why tell me that?"

"My instincts have always served me well. I sense you and I are of similar minds on the matter, and I need to know what's happening beyond my city walls. I can't afford to wait for a better opportunity when one may never come. Where are you from?"

"Clodhill." It's much safer than saying Jodpirn and close enough to the truth it shouldn't alert her to any falsehood. "What is your plan?"

Suvi tilts her head and purses her lips. "Right for the heart. I should've expected as much. Are you any good at keeping secrets?"

I shrug. "Haven't had any to keep."

"The humans in the south will be annihilated without my help. We could use a mixling like you, with powers like yours—"

"How do you know about my magic?"

If she's bothered by being interrupted, she doesn't show it. "I sense your power, as you sense mine, though I'm probably much better at it. I've had lessons and practice, whereas your ability is raw and untrained. There aren't many wielders as strong as us." Her tone shifts, becoming more serious. "You could warn them. You could lead them to safety."

A numb sensation passes through me, followed on its heels by a startling jolt of purpose. I'm no leader, but maybe I could assist. I could save people. My jaw hangs open as the idea fights for life in my mind.

"I can help you," she offers. "If you'll agree to help me."

"How do I know you're telling the truth?"

She extends her hand, skin sparkling with the luminescence of the fae, so like Jindal's, unadorned by jewelry, nails naturally shining, not painted. "Take it. Read me."

I blink. Can I do that? But I know I can. I've done it by accident more times than I can count, but when it's happened before, I rejected the info and pretended not to know because it felt so personal.

This time, I let it happen.

Her hand is warm in mine. Soft. Palm to palm and face-to-face, we meet each other's gazes. Her words are honest, and her intent is pure. She wants to end the suffering and injustice humans face in our realm. She sends me a memory, and I swim in it, dazed.

A little fae princess and her human nursemaid, outside in a flower garden, warm sunlight on their faces. Laughter and love.

The same little girl, her face beet red, with tears streaking down her cheeks. "Bring her back. Momma! Momma!"

The nursemaid being hauled away by guards, fighting to return to her charge, but to no avail.

My heart aches for both of them.

The queen, Aurielle—for who else could she be—harsh and angry. "Cease this at once, Suvi. That woman is not your mother."

The little girl's cries only grow louder and more desperate. "Momma!"

The vision fades, and the girl, all grown up, stands before me. "I want to help."

I believe her with my whole soul. "So do I."

Chapter Sixteen

Jindal

It hasn't rained in ten days, and the crops are flagging. I filled my morning fussing over the rain barrels and adjusting the flow of the remaining water to our irrigation system to wet the most vulnerable plants. A little dash of my magic doesn't hurt either.

But no matter how much work there is to be done, I make time to fly south every day at lunch and check the roads. Then again before dusk for one last look, with hope in my heart that this time, I'll see Rahz astride Magna, headed my way, almost home.

No such luck.

It's been one month, one week, and two days since Rahz left. Any minute now, he'll return to me, and we can put this foul business behind us.

Back at the farm, I spend my afternoon pulling weeds, which somehow thrive even when the vegetable crop around them is all wilted and puny. But the poor plants won't have to wait long. I smell rain in the air. It's coming. Perhaps tonight, perhaps tomorrow, but water is on the way.

And hopefully, so is Rahz.

In the end, Rahz and the rain come at once.

The sprinkling is light, misting the air and making my wings sticky. I've flown to the best vantage point by which to see the place where the southern road disappears into the vast old-growth forest, but I may have to walk back. Much wetter, and flight won't be an option.

But that's all right. I have less work to do today with the encroaching weather, so I have time on my hands.

I sit under the petals of a massive blue titan lily, my back against its sturdy stem, and settle in to wait. Snacking on toasted nuts and a slice of bread I made all by myself, I watch the horizon for two men on horseback.

As boys, Rahz and I would sometimes come here, looking for gargoyles, spies, or wayward princesses in need of rescue. Anything more exciting than our regular lives. We only ever saw other farmers, travelers, and merchants, but each was exciting in their own way.

When we were older, we'd sometimes continue down the road to the cover of the forest to steal some private time for wandering hands and pleasured sighs.

Most of my memories were formed with Rahz, which is why I've felt so unsettled without him. As though the air is too thin to lift me, the ground too hard to tread upon, our bed too empty to sleep in alone. Rahz is the anchor to my ship. Without him, I drift, aimless and lacking purpose.

Of course Bessa and Bird have been great company. Deepening our relationships has kept me afloat. But I won't feel whole again until Rahz is by my side.

When my food is gone and my hind end has gone numb, I stand to stretch my limbs and shake out my wings. They're dry enough to fly home, but first, I cast another hopeful look down the road.

And I don't believe my eyes.

Two men. Two horses. One hundred beats per minute of my sprinting heart!

I'm in the air before making the decision to fly, racing toward them as fast as my wings can carry me. I spot the moment Rahz sees me, even though he's still far away. The change in his posture, the lengthening of his spine, and the tap of his heels along Magna's flanks to urge her into a gallop.

We race toward each other, my laughter ringing as joy fills my chest with warmth.

Rahz slows Magna in just enough time to leap off her back and catch me as I barrel into him, knocking us both to the damp ground. His laughter joins mine, singing the sweet chorus of our happy reunion.

Our lips meet in a hurried rush. Rahz holds me tight as I bury my fingers in his mane of silver hair, breathing him in and relishing his familiar scent.

We're still kissing when Falen catches up. "Should I wait? Will you two be coming up for air anytime soon?"

With no small amount of reluctance, I climb off Rahz, grab his hand, and help him to his feet. He wraps his big arm around my shoulders and tugs me against his side into that spot I fit so well in it's as if it were meant only for me.

"Hello, Falen." I offer him a smile with spit-slick lips. "Maybe you could go on ahead? I'm sure Bird will be thrilled you're home."

"I'll do that." He nods to Rahz. "Tomorrow night at the quarry?"

Rahz returns the gesture. "I'll see you then."

I'm bursting with questions and curiosity, but as Falen rides off, my mouth is put to better use when Rahz kisses me again.

"What's happening at the quarry?" I mumble against his lips and around his tongue.

"I have so much to tell you." He lifts me off my feet and strides back the way he came toward the cover of the forest, clucking for Magna to follow. "After."

I wrap my legs around his waist and squeeze. "After," I agree easily. I've missed him so much. I need to have him now, to reconnect body and soul. Whatever news he has from the capital, tales from the journey, and plans at the quarry can wait another hour.

Or two.

My delight titters out in a giggle against the sensitive skin of his throat, where I've locked my lips, intending to leave my mark.

Rahz picks up speed, so strong as he carries me under the cover of the tree line. "You might not like it," he mutters, tilting his head to give me better access. "In fact, I'm sure you're not going to like it."

That gives me pause. A chord of worry strikes my gut. I pull back to look him in the eyes. "Are you all right?"

"Yes."

"And you're safe?"

The tiniest bit of hesitation. "Safe enough."

His answer ratchets up my worry. "Rahz."

"After?" His hungry gaze lights a fire in my blood. "I need you so much."

"Yes." I bob my head with the enthusiasm of a man about to get railed. "Have me, please. I need you too."

I slide down his body, and he lets me go, sets me on my own two feet, but I have other plans. I push him until his back hits the solid support of a sturdy tree trunk and drop to my knees to unlace his breeches and tug out my prize.

His cock is half-hard in my hand already, and I intend to

stiffen him up the rest of the way with my mouth, but when I lick my lips, he places his hand over mine.

"Um, maybe not that?"

I blink. "Huh?"

"I haven't washed, not properly, not in days. And my magic doesn't do the job as well as soap and water."

He's wrong. His magic works fine. "I want to." The natural smells of his body are only more of a turn-on, not less. "I want you as you are. Just like this. I want you any way I can have you. Always."

Rahz's eyes shine wetly. "You really mean that, don't you?"

"Of course. You're my Rahz, and I love you more than anything. Can I?"

His shaky nod is all the permission I need. I swallow him with gusto. The feel of him, heavy on my tongue, stretching my lips wide, wrings a moan from deep in my throat.

"Ah, Jin!"

When he says my name that way, it sounds like begging. And I covet making Rahz beg.

I might have been a little overeager, but he's so good it's impossible to hold back. Rahz's fingers tangle in my hair, and that's even better.

Everything is wet and slick and hot. I suck my fill of him, then return for more. My hands clench on his thighs. I don't need them for this. I'm going to make him come with just my mouth, and if the desperate, whimpering noises pouring from him are anything to go by, it's not going to take long.

Stars, I've been dreaming of this for ages, sucking him. It's even better than I'd imagined. I use my tongue to lave the length of his shaft, to swirl around the tip, and to pleasure the bundle of nerves beneath his crown. I relish every moan he makes and delight in the tug of his fingers in my hair.

Rahz thrusts his hips. He's aching for a rhythm already, so I give him one, moving my head along with his motions. His cock throbs in my mouth, and mine twitches in tandem, eager to join the fun.

"Please, Jin. Don't stop." His thighs tremble under my palms.

I relax my throat and let him use me as he likes because whatever he likes, I love. He tightens his grip, pulling at my scalp in a way that makes me shiver. My cock hangs full and heavy between my legs, and it's all I can do not to stroke it myself. It'll be worth the wait.

I don't have to wait long.

Rahz's hips stutter, and he expands impossibly bigger, forcing my throat wide. As he comes, he cries out, music to my ears, shooting inside me like a geyser while holding me in place to swallow around him. It's pure bliss after so long without, and I want all of it, greedy thing that I am.

I milk the last bits of pleasure from him until he's wrung out, leaning heavily on the tree and panting. Even then I don't stop, but I slow my motions to a soft, caressing nuzzle, breathing in his scent. The scent he somehow thought I wouldn't like, but I treasure.

He takes his hands from my hair and cups my cheeks, tilting my face upward. "You have no idea how much I needed that."

A chuckle escapes. "I think I do. I need you too."

"Hmm? What do you need, Jin? What do you want?"

"Anything!" I let go of his thighs and unfasten my pants. "No, wait. Your hand. That's what I want. I'm so sick of mine after weeks without yours."

He kneels in front of me and grins. His face is flushed pink and glistening with the mist still falling all around us. "At least *you* had your own hand. I've been sharing camp with Falen for weeks. I've barely had a minute alone to take care of things."

"Poor Rahz." I kiss him. Our lips slip into the familiar dance easily. "I wish you hadn't had to go. I missed you so badly."

"And I you." He grips my neglected cock and strokes, fingers and palm already gloriously slick. One long slide of his hand, and I'm hurtling toward bliss. "So hard for me," he rumbles, his breath warming the shell of my ear. "So ready."

"Yes." I lean into him, letting him bear my weight. It's awkward like this, the angle, face-to-face, but I don't care. I want to press my skin against his, my smooth cheek sliding along the bristles of his rough one. I wish we were naked. His chest expands against mine, and I curse the layers of cloth separating us.

I wrap my arms around his big shoulders, and he curls his free one around my waist. In the negligible space between us, he works my cock. His hand on me again feels so good. So right. After this, we'll rush home, and I'll beg him to fuck me in our bed, make the sheets smell like us again instead of just me. I can't wait.

Pressure rises with a tingling sensation that makes my lips part and my toes curl. I suck the lobe of his ear into my mouth and moan around it. He's an expert at this. Knows me so well. Just how I like it. How fast and how hard, and with that perfect twist of his wrist at the top.

I close my eyes. My balls draw tight as the inevitability of release crashes over me. I tighten my arms around Rahz, squeezing him close. My muscles flutter and quake as I spill my seed in his palm.

My breath comes in damp gasps against his ear. His hand gentles around my cock, soothing me down from the high. I never want to be parted from him. I want to stay like this forever, holding each other, warm, even in the gentle fall of rain.

"Feel good?" His lips move against my cheek. A smile.

"Perfect." I kiss the point of his ear because it's right there, and it's so cute, and I have to be touching him anywhere I can.

"Me too." He turns his face for a proper kiss, and I meet him.

We're wet, disheveled, and our knees are filthy, but I couldn't have dreamed up a better reunion. To have him back in my arms is all I'll ever need.

"I got you something." With a flourish of his hand a wave of his magic tidies us up. Then he shuffles down and sits on his haunches.

I scoot back enough to watch what he's doing. "You did?"

He reaches behind his neck and pulls forward a lovely necklace. A stunning orange stone with artfully twisted golden lattice in a circle around it, holding it in place, dangles from the chain, or rather two chains. Two gold chains.

As he removes the piece, he presses just so, and the stone separates from its casing. Two necklaces coming together to form one.

"For you. The jewel matches your eyes but could never outshine them." Rahz hands me the stone. I love the weight of it in my palm. "And I'll wear what's left. Because I'm always here to hold you."

Warmth floods my chest. It's so sappy and so perfect. "I love them." I hand mine back. "Put it on me, please?"

"My pleasure." Rahz's fingers are gentle as he clasps the new necklace around my neck. The jewel rests beneath my collarbones, a comforting weight, already warmed from his body.

"Thank you."

"You're welcome." He presses a kiss on my brow.

I hold the stone in my palm, loving it. Loving that he picked this for me. "Yours is beautiful too." And it is. A simple golden circle of delicately twisted gold. It suits him, and I like knowing there's a space for me just there, over his heart.

"You're so sweet." Another kiss. To catch up on all the ones we've missed. "I want to hear everything. All about your trip. Every day and every night."

His expression clouds as he takes a deep breath. My mood clouds with it.

"Unless it's bad. Is it bad? Well, I mean, I still want to know, obviously, but I don't want to upset you if you'd rather not talk about it, and you've had such a long journey, and—"

Rahz stops me with a quick kiss. "You don't upset me. You never could. There's a lot to tell, not all of it bad. But I'm afraid you aren't going to like some of what I'll say."

That sounds ominous. "Tell me, then. Let's get it over with and find out."

"In the dirt? In the rain?"

"Why not?"

He clucks for Magna, who's wandered off to graze. "Because I'm this close to one of Bessa's homemade meals, and I'd rather us talk at home, warm and dry in our loft."

Actually, that does sound better. Rahz is right, as always. "Yes, let's do that. Your plan."

I'm so grateful to have him back at my side.

I'll never let him leave me ever again.

Chapter Seventeen

Rahz

WE HEAD FIRST TO THE STABLES TO TAKE CARE OF
Magna and help her recover from the journey. She's done so
well. I couldn't be happier to have her as my horse. She tosses her
head and snorts proudly, preening as if she knows what I'm
thinking.

After she's been properly pampered, we visit my mother to
let her know I'm home safe. Like Jindal, she wants to hear the
whole story right away, but she sees I'm tired. It's easy to
convince her to wait until tomorrow, once I'm fresh from sleep. I
promise to come back first thing in the morning, and with that,
she lets us go.

Next, we stop in at Jindal's cottage, where I receive a warm
hug and a swat to my rump for taking so long from Bessa. Then
a gruff, "Welcome back, lad," with a jerky nod from Jindal's
father.

As I'd hoped, Bessa turns to the kitchen to put together a

meal for Jin and me to take to the loft, but first, apricot pastries are shoved into my hands to hold me over before supper.

"Oh, Bessa," I mumble, my mouth stuffed full, "how I've missed you."

"You mean how you've missed my baking." She winks. "Don't lie."

"I missed that too, but I missed you more." I've got presents for her in my bags, but I didn't think to get Jindal's father anything, so I'll wait until we're alone to give them to her. A new apron in her favorite color, bright yellow, and a cooking spice called saffron that I've never heard of but smells as good as can be.

Jindal carries the tray of food, and I carry my bags as we make the trek across the field to our own little private space in the barn. The rain has stopped, and it's dark out but not so dark we can't see. Sparkling bugs glow in clusters over the windswept grasses. I take a deep breath of country fresh air and smile. Smells like home.

If only I could stay.

My heart is heavy with the news I must share with Jindal. I can only hope he'll understand. That he'll choose to come with me. But I know he won't want to leave Jodpirn. Not while his mother still sleeps. Maybe not ever.

We climb the ladder to our loft and hoist up our items with a pulley system rigged long ago, when we were still boys. The savory scent of Bessa's meat pies has my mouth watering for a taste. With the meal spread on our little table between us, we sit on worn cushions and tuck in.

I moan. "It's even better than I remembered."

A grin lights Jindal's face. "Bessa must have magic of her own, even though she's never admitted as much."

"I won't argue." The meat is tender, and the vegetables are perfectly spiced—potato, onion, and peas all stirred in a creamy gravy sauce.

Jindal is itching for me to start talking, but I'm so hungry. He waits about as patiently as Jindal ever does anything, which is to say, not very patiently at all. He's a twitching bundle of movement across from me, wings fluttering and settling, fluttering and settling, all while he shifts from one hip to the other, barely keeping from demanding the story.

It's cute and familiar, and he's trying so hard I take pity on him.

"Shall I talk as I eat?" My pie is halfway gone, and the edge has worn from my hunger.

"Please." His orange gaze lands on me eagerly. Is he as nervous about this as I am?

I start by relaying our journey. This is the easy part. Descriptions of each town, the magnificent views, the forests, the flowers, the people, the animals, the river, and the ferry. These are all good memories. Folks were kind to us on our travels. Mixlings are generally respected by the fae for our combined heritage, our magic, which is often superior, our contributions to the bloodlines, our physical strength. Humans have none of these advantages bestowed on me by the accident of birth.

Jindal listens intently, enraptured as I spin the tale. He can't imagine a river so big a boat would be needed to cross it, much less a boat big enough to ferry horses, wagons, livestock, and people all at once. Around here, the largest river spans no more than forty paces across and rises no higher than a man's shoulders, even in the deepest parts. It's easily swimmable, but there's no need because we've built bridges. The Onyx is so big, though, no bridge could span it.

I tell him of Lemossin, the hustle and bustle of the capital city, the grandeur of Ralossi Palace when viewed by the main streets, the variety of food at the markets. More of the easy memories.

It's harder to explain how people talk there, how free they are with their hostility toward the humans of Irondale and the revolt. How they've come to expect more fighting. How they seem to welcome it as an infestation of bugs to be squashed.

Jindal's eyes grow wide and darken. "Are they all like that? So prejudiced?"

"I hope not, but certainly the ones speaking the loudest are all like that. Which worries me. And the humans who work in Lemossin slink around quickly, ducking in shadows like they don't want to be seen."

"Like they're afraid."

"Yes. And for good reason. There are so many of them. If they did rebel, I don't think they'd be conquered as easily as the fae seem to think, but they aren't organized. As is, they have no power."

"I'm so glad we live here instead. Where we're safe. Where Bessa and your mother are safe."

For now. But I can't bring myself to say the words. I don't want to frighten Jindal any more than is strictly necessary. "There's more."

"Go on." Jindal has stopped eating and pushes his plate toward me.

I shove my empty plate aside, happy to finish his as well. I go on eating as I talk, which somehow makes the next part easier to get out, telling him of my and Falen's plan inside the palace and how I used my magic to sneak away.

Concern is written all over Jindal's face. "But you hate using mind magic."

He's not wrong. "I could think of no other way. But I did get lucky." I explain how I caught the attention of Princess Suvi, and of our secret meetings.

"That's what took us so long. We had to stay in Lemossin several extra days, so Suvi could catch me up on everything I'd need to know, so I could meet the right people, so we could plan what to do."

Jindal's face has frozen, his expression iced over. Only his eyelids move as he blinks.

"She has soldiers in place in Willowood, just before Irondale, a troop loyal only to her, with two mages already in their ranks, but none so strong as me. If I were to join them—"

"You can't," Jin wails, looking shocked by his outburst as though it took him by surprise.

"I must." I knew this part was going to be awful. "If the queen is allowed to raise an army, an army she plans to fill with mixlings who are more capable both physically and magically, there'll be no stopping her. Aurielle will slaughter all the rebels, man, woman, child. She cares not who's innocent. But Suvi's troop is already formed. We can get there first. Warn them and help move them to safety. You can't kill what you can't find. Then Aurielle will be forced to consider peace talks. That's all Suvi wants. Peace."

Jindal is shaking his head, and I'm not sure how much he's hearing me anymore. "But not you, Rahz. Not you. You're safe here."

"Jin." I put my spoon down and take his hand in mine. "Those people need help. They could die. And I have a chance to be a part of saving them."

He lets out a sad whimper.

The rise and fall of his chest quickens, a telltale sign he's beginning to panic. I pull him to my side. "You know I can protect myself. And Suvi has a solid plan in place. She doesn't want fighting if it can be avoided."

"But you just got back." His voice is quiet, and his hand is oddly limp in mine. "I can't lose you again."

Here it is. The big ask. I brace myself. "Come with me. You're clever and agile and fast. You can help us."

Our eyes lock, his getting more watery by the second. He parts his lips, but words don't come.

"It won't be forever, but we must go soon. The timing is

crucial. Suvi wanted to send me there directly, but I insisted on returning to tell you first. To ask you to join me. I hated being parted from you, Jin. I missed you every moment."

The tears spill over his lids. There was never any chance of him holding them back. He flings himself into my lap and clings to me. "Don't leave."

I hold him, and we rock. "I must."

"You could get hurt."

"The risk is worth the reward. Those people are helpless."

"But this...fighting, war...this is your nightmare."

He's right. I've tossed and turned over dreams of battle in night terrors for years, but it doesn't matter. "I have to go."

"When?"

A sad sigh swallows me. "Not tomorrow morning but the next."

"So soon? Why you?" He persists, miserable, his shoulders shaking. I squeeze him close. "Why couldn't she send anyone else but you?"

"She's been looking for someone like me for quite some time before we met. It's my magic she needs, my magic, and of course my belief in her cause. She'll make a good queen one day, Jindal. Aurielle can't keep the throne forever, and Suvi will usher in the changes Luminia deserves. I could play a small part in that. For the good of all of us."

Jindal shakes as he cries, his face damp where he's buried it in my neck. Oh, I love him so. To cause him pain like this is agony, but whereas Jindal has always struggled to see the greater good, I cannot pretend I don't know what the right thing to do is. I rub circles on his back under his wings, trying to soothe him, though I know he can't be soothed.

"I'm sorry, Rahz. I'm sorry. I'm so, so..."

"You're fine as you are, my love. Cry all you need. I may join you this time. I feel it coming."

He glances up, his face all splotchy and sad. My eyes water. Usually, I can hold back tears. This time, I can't.

One droplet escapes, streaking a wet trail down my cheek.

Jin swipes it gently with his thumb. "I don't know what to do. I can't let you go, but neither can I demand you stay. That would be unfair to you. Yet I can't join you either." He drops his gaze. "My mother is here."

That's what I was afraid of. I wish he'd come. We belong together. But I won't tear him from the one hope he's held on to as long as I've known him. That his mother will wake and love him for who he is in a way his father can't. But she could be dormant for a hundred more cycles—we have no way of knowing—and the humans need my help now.

"I understand, my love." Tugging him closer, I take comfort in his warmth. "I'll support your choice to stay behind."

He collapses again, head on my shoulder, sobbing. To be honest, I expected this, and I hate to be the cause of it, but we need this moment, just as we've needed all the ones that have come before. Just as we need all the moments yet to be.

I kiss his ear and then murmur into it. "Our souls are connected, Jindal, forever, and though distance may part our bodies for a time, nothing can separate our souls. One day, this will be nothing but one more memory along with all the rest."

We go to bed, and my heart breaks as he cries himself to sleep.

Chapter Eighteen

JINDAL

RAHZ HAS GONE TO VISIT WITH HIS MOTHER, AND though my father gave me the stink-eye for it, I've abandoned my work to seek out Bessa. Rahz has given me permission to tell her everything, and it's all I can think about. Maybe she will know what to say to get him to stay.

Bessa will understand. She'll help me.

As I race to her doorstep, people look at me funny. Probably because I haven't really stopped crying since I woke this morning. At first, I was thrilled to have Rahz back at my side again, and then, as reality vanquished my dream world, I was distraught that he'll be leaving again so soon. I must look a mess, bedraggled and puffy-eyed.

I barely stop to knock on Bessa's door. Barging in would be rude, and though I'm not a child anymore, it's all I can do to wait for her to answer.

She opens it, gets one look at my face, and tugs me inside. I fall apart all over again in her arms.

"He's leaving me," I sob wetly on her shoulder. We are of the same height, but she's built stronger than I am, and thank goodness for that because she's holding me up.

"What's happened?" She rubs my back. "There, there, calm down enough so you can talk to me."

I've never been good at calming down. Being here with her, in her loving embrace, only makes me cry harder. I don't know why. When I'm sad and people are nice to me, I lose all composure.

Bessa shuffles us over to the lounge in the living room side of her cottage. It's all the same room, really: living, cooking, and dining. Through the doorway is a bedroom, and that's the extent of her little home.

We flop onto the seat as one, and she lets me cry it out, all the while patting me and murmuring soothing words into my ear.

Am I too old for this?

Yes.

Do I care?

Absolutely not, though I'll probably be embarrassed about it later. I managed to hold myself together enough to send Rahz on his way to visit his mother. I didn't want him worrying about me during his time with her. But now I'm lost, drowning in my fears. Being alone, losing Rahz, everything changing.

Change is hard. It's the unknown wrapped up in the ambiguous, and I crave the comfort of the familiar.

When I've stopped wailing enough to talk, Bessa teases the story from me bit by bit.

"Come now, love. From the beginning, please. Whatever it is cannot be all that bad."

"Oh, but it is!" My throat hurts from all the crying, and my voice is scratchy. "Rahz is leaving again."

Bessa's brows crease. She pushes my messy hair behind my

ears. "Slowly, and don't leave anything out. He must have good reasons. What did he say?"

I pour everything out to her like a river plummeting down a waterfall. In the telling, my tears return. She never stops coddling me, patting my knee, and encouraging me to keep going. Whatever I've done to deserve a woman like Bessa in my life, it hasn't been enough.

"Oh, Bessa, I'm sorry to burden you with this. I have no one else to go to, and it's too big to keep inside me."

"Of course, love. That's foul news to swallow, it is. But, Jin, we've seen this coming, haven't we? Is it really that much of a surprise that our dear Rahz wants to help those people?"

"Let someone else help them."

"Now, now, don't be rash. Rahz is strong. He's clever and kind and powerful but most of all, Rahz has a huge heart. You should know because he's given so much of it to you."

I sniffle and nod, feeling all the more pitiful.

"It's time you had a good long think. A hard think." When I open my mouth, she shushes me and squeezes my knee. "No, listen. Your feelings are important, and I'm not blaming you for them. I'm always here for you, and I understand you're scared. Let those emotions flow, but not only for yourself. Think of Rahz. Think of his mother. His *human* mother. Who could just as well have been born in Irondale. Who could easily have been wrapped up in this mess. Who is vulnerable if the tide turns against us. What's a boy like Rahz with a heart like his supposed to do? Sit back and watch as the humans in the south are threatened?"

The air sweeps from my lungs in a painful rush.

She's right. Of course she is. My chest hollows. I gaze at the woman I love most in the world, the one who's always taken care of me, and who's taking care of me still.

Human.

Like Rahz's sweet mother.

Like the people of Irondale.

I can't breathe. I've been so stupid. So selfish. Not to see it before now. A threat to one is a threat to all.

Bessa collects me back into her arms. I squeeze my eyes shut against the world and hug her fiercely. She lets me cry all over again. "Oh, Jindal, forever my little boy, you're going to be all right."

I hate myself at this moment. How terrible I am. How thoughtless. "He asked me to go with him."

Bessa shifts enough to look me in the eyes. "And you said no?" Her surprise shocks me a little.

"Because of Mother..." I let the thought trail off. My mother is sleeping. Has always been sleeping. Might be sleeping still when all of this is said and done.

"Your mother, when she wakes, will love you no matter what. Whether you've waited here or forged a life of your own somewhere else."

I'm holding the hem of Bessa's worn apron, fingering a loose seam as my world unravels around me and begins anew. "I should go."

"You"—she catches my chin and gives me the most loving look, a look that melts my heart—"should think. Don't react, don't lash out, just sit with your thoughts. Can you do that for me?"

"Yes." The word might come out in a scared whisper, but I mean it. "I'll do it."

"At the river. Alone. Don't drag Rahz from his mum for this."

"No, I wouldn't."

"Have you eaten?"

I shake my head.

"Let me pack you something." She disentangles herself from me and heads to the cupboards. "Thinking goes best with a full stomach."

Though I'm reeling inside, I smile. Bessa wouldn't let a soul go hungry if it were in her power to feed them. I have no appetite, but maybe I'll feel differently later.

She puts together a little sack for me and shoves this into my hands. "I'll be here if you need me. Right here. I'm not going anywhere. But you can do this all by yourself."

Her faith in me flushes my face. Heat warms my cheeks and chest. "Thank you."

"I love you, Jinny."

"I love you too, Bessa. I'm sorry—"

"Aught. None of that. You have nothing to apologize for." She wipes my face with her apron and kisses my cheek. "Tell Rahz to come see me before he goes. He'll need provisions."

That almost wrings a chuckle out of me. Almost.

In a way, I leave Bessa's cottage feeling worse than when I arrived, but in another way, I feel stronger.

Maybe I can be the person Rahz and Bessa seem to think I am. A better person. A person more like they are.

Chapter Nineteen

Rahz

THE HEAT OF THE DAY CREEPS IN ON US, BUT MOTHER and I stay comfortable in the shade, rocking on the porch swing that overlooks our small garden. The air smells of flower blossoms and the booming mint crop that's threatening to take over the rest of the patch. I make a note to trim it back. One last little thing I can do for Mum before I go.

But not yet because this is nice. The rhythmic creaking of rope against wood as we swing lulls me to calm. Today is the first —and likely the only—day I have without any travel in some time.

We're enjoying a companionable silence. Well, not silent. She's singing, which may also be contributing to my delightfully drowsy state. The tune she hums is melancholy but lovely in its way. A lullaby, though not one she ever sang to me. Her lullabies were always of the cheerful variety. This tune is somber, but her voice is soothing and rich nonetheless.

I've explained everything to her, and though she worries for my safety, as Jindal does, she understands why I must go. She's given me her blessing, and I'm at peace with my decision. All that's left is to enjoy this time together before I head back to Jindal to comfort him as best I can.

Early this evening, I'll meet with Falen at the quarry. He's not coming to Irondale with me, but his family has armor and a sword he said I can have. Not that a sword will do me much good. I haven't been properly trained. The few fencing lessons we had in our youth I've rightly forgotten. But Suvi says there will be time to train with her troops if I so desire, and I do. Though I'm not planning to fight with a sword but with my magic, it's a skill I'll enjoy learning. And I'm going to need to stay busy, or missing Jindal will send me spiraling.

In addition to the armor and sword, Falen is bringing a horse for Jindal. I asked him to pick out the sweetest, most mild-mannered gelding he could find. Wishful thinking on my part that Jindal would decide to come with me and therefore need a horse, but better to be prepared.

Suvi was generous enough to send along money for the animal. Jindal will get to keep him, even though he's not coming, and with any luck, the horse will comfort him while I'm away. I worry about him being alone here. Even though he has friends and Bessa, I know he'll be lonely without me. And sad. I hate to think of Jindal being sad.

Speaking of Jindal...

He comes flying over the back gate in a flutter of wings and abandon, hollering my name.

"Rahz!" He's winded, breathless as the words come tumbling out. "Rahz, I'm coming with you. I'll come with you. We won't be alone, neither of us, because I'm coming too."

He lands, half kneeling and half flopped over my shoulder, on my lap, sending our porch swing rocking wildly. I grab him, confused. Hope tries desperately to bloom in my chest, but I tamp it down until I'm sure he's saying what I think he's saying.

Mother is smiling, watching us, and holding on to the rail of the swing for dear life lest Jin send us all hurtling to the ground with his unbridled excitement.

"I'm coming with you." He holds my face in his hands, realizes we're not alone, and returns my mother's smile with an answering grin. "Hello, Ms. Starling."

"Hullo, Jinny." She pats his arm. She's used to him. His wild nature, his enthusiasm and flightiness, his silly whims, and his sweet words. All the things that made me love him. "Shall I leave you two alone, then?"

"You don't have to," he says a bit more calmly.

She rises from the swing. "I think I will, though."

"Sorry for interrupting." Jindal has the courtesy to look sheepish.

"Don't be." She pats his arm again and kisses his temple. "There's no need, and I'm glad you came."

When we're alone, he shuffles into her spot while still managing to stay half in my lap.

"What about your mother?" I trust Jindal with my life, but I don't trust this quick turnabout, not yet. It feels too good to be true.

"I've thought about that. I've been thinking over it for hours." The longing in his eyes burns bright. "And I have to believe my mother will love me one day, no matter where I am. But *you* love me now. And I love you. My place is by your side. Your fight is my fight."

I'm stunned. It's what I wanted to hear but never really expected him to say.

"I'm sorry I didn't realize as much right away. I was overwhelmed. And afraid." He glances down. "My mind doesn't work very well when I feel like that. But Bessa helped me calm down. She helped me to see."

I tip his head up. "You're really willing to leave Jodpirn for me?"

He nods. I almost don't recognize the determined expression on his face. "For you, yes, but not only for you. For the humans who need us. For the princess who has vowed to help them. For your mum and for Bessa. Because it's the right thing for me to do. I want to go with you."

My heart takes up so much space in my chest I can't breathe. I'm so proud of him, my Jin, my love, yet I'm sad for him too. That he'll need to leave the side of his sleeping mother in order to come along, and such a long way at that. "Are you sure? I meant it when I said I understood why you needed to stay behind."

"I know you did." He squirms closer, draping one leg heavily over mine. "I appreciate that, truly, but I want to be someone my mother can be proud of when she wakes. Someone more like you, who thinks of others first rather than needing to be dragged over the coals before realizing what's right under their nose."

The truth of his decision sinks in, along with a rush of warmth. I grab him, yank him in for a chest-crushing hug, and bury my face in his neck. "You're allowed to take all the time you need. Don't ever let me rush you."

"Thank you, but honestly, maybe you should," he wheezes out, and I let off on the pressure a bit. "I can be dreadfully slow sometimes."

"You're perfect as you are." I kiss his nose, as I used to do all those years ago when we first started kissing.

His response is a damp row of warm kisses planted along my jaw. "And you're so good to me. I will be just as good to you. We belong together."

I couldn't agree more.

JINDAL

IT'S EARLY EVENING, AND I'M RIDING PILLION BEHIND Rahz, my arms looped around his sturdy waist. Magna's steady gait rocks us together, and I lean forward against his back, enjoying the closeness.

Could I fly and spare Magna the extra burden? Yes. But my stomach is queasy. I've been feeling funny all evening, like I've got fluff in my head where my brain should be. It's a sensation as though remembering the wispy hints of a dream without being able to recall the whole thing.

Maddening, odd, and unsettling.

So I take comfort in Rahz's proximity, my head resting between his shoulder blades as he guides Magna onward. He assures me my added weight is nothing to her for so short a trip. She's such a strong horse, surefooted and true.

We're headed to meet Falen, who's bringing me a horse of my own for the journey to Irondale, one paid for by the royal princess herself. I don't know how to feel about accepting such a generous gift from such an important lady, but I can't help but be a little excited. I love animals, and though I don't ride often, I do enjoy it when given the chance.

As we crest the little hill overlooking the oval rim of the rock quarry, I peer over Rahz's shoulder. Falen and Bird are already there. His mare Chestnut grazes on the tall roadside grasses, and next to her is a large spotted gelding with a flowing mane and tail the color of freshly whipped cream.

"Gorgeous," I murmur into Rahz's ear. For a moment, I'm so taken with my first look at the horse I forget my muddled brain and queasy belly.

"Yes, very," Rahz agrees. "And perfect for you. You'll be taller than me for once." He chuckles, his stomach vibrating beneath my palms.

"That'll make a nice change."

We wave and say hello to our friends, then dismount to meet our new family member. He ambles over to me, eyes bright and clear, a curious expression on his long, speckled face.

I love him already.

"His name's Briar." Falen gives Rahz his reins. "He's a good boy."

"Hello, handsome." I stroke the soft nose of the sturdy gray roan. He snuffle-snorts and turns his big face into my hand. "You and I are going to be good friends."

"He likes you," says Falen. "Here, give him this. I brought bribes, just in case, but it looks like you don't need them."

Falen hands me a big purple carrot, and I hold it out for Briar to take. "Here you are, the first of many."

While Briar happily chomps on the treat, Magna noses Rahz's shoulder for one of her own.

"Sorry, girl." Rahz scratches her neck. "You already like me, so I didn't bring any bribes."

Falen ponies up another carrot for Magna and one for Chestnut as well. Briar looks so big next to the others. I admire his dappled coat, hardly believing he's mine to care for. He will make the long journey so much easier. No way could I fly that far on my own.

We're gathered by the eastern rim, a good place to be alone, just the four of us, for this meeting. The others can't know where we're headed or who we're planning to help. It's all very hush-hush.

Our cover story is that Rahz was so enchanted with Lemossin he simply had to bring me there for an extended visit. After securing temporary work for both of us in the capital and extra help for Father on the farm, the deed was done.

I feel guilty over it, but I'm not telling Father until the last possible moment. He'll try to talk me out of it, and when that fails, he'll put his foot down and forbid me to go, which will also fail. I'm an adult and free to make my own choices, though I'm sure he'll feel otherwise. I don't want to fight, so I'm putting it off as long as possible.

Vander, of all people, is coordinating help for the farm. How Rahz convinced him, I don't know, but it probably has to do with a bigger share of the harvest for his family. And by going to him for help, we shoot any rumors he might have started otherwise in the foot. Rahz is clever like that.

"When are you leaving?" asks Bird.

"Tomorrow morning," says Rahz. "I wish it didn't have to be so soon, but there's no time to spare."

I lean in to give Bird a hug. "Thank you for being such a good friend to me while we were alone."

"Same to you." She squeezes me tight. "Be careful on your journey, and return to us as soon as you can." Her eyes shift to Rahz. "You'll keep him safe, won't you?"

"Always," he says, and I shift from her arms back into his.

"Jodpirn won't be the same with you and Rahz both gone. You're such staples in our community. What will we do without you?"

Rahz huffs. "Vander will have to get off his lazy bottom and help out for a change. Promise you'll keep him busy for us."

Her grin says she'll take this task to heart. "Perhaps I'll start by accidentally leaving the pig pen open. Who better to wrangle swine than one of their own?"

"I love this plan." Imagining Vander covered in mud and pig scraps brings no shortage of delight.

We're all laughing as my name in a frantic tone is called loudly from the other side of the hill.

"Jindal. Jindal!"

Is that Father? I've never heard him sound quite so animated. Why would he follow me here?

"Jindal!" He bursts over the crest in a flutter of gray wings and ragged mania.

I reach for Rahz's hand, my muscles tensing. In memory, the only time he's used our family bond to track me down somewhere was because I was in trouble for something. Suddenly, I'm a young child again, slipping behind Rahz for protection.

"Jindal," he puffs, out of breath, one hand clenching his chest as he lands in front of our startled group.

"Yes, Father?" My voice is small. Frightened.

His dark eyes are blazing, locked onto mine as he utters the four words I've yearned to hear all my life.

"Your mother is awake."

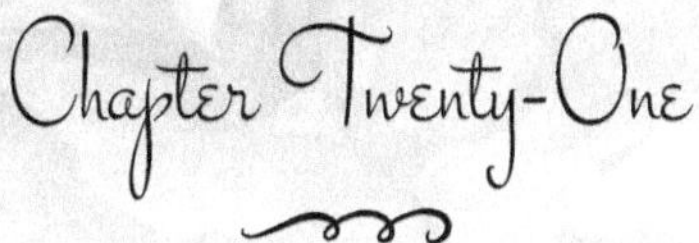

Chapter Twenty-One

Jindal

A WAVE OF CONFUSION SPILLS OVER ME, FOLLOWED BY a longing so deep I'm drowning in it. I'm afraid to believe him. Has he somehow discovered my plans? Is this just a tactic to keep me here?

Or...

Is my mother really awake? Finally? After all these years. "How do you know?"

He rolls his eyes and scowls. "Don't question me, boy. She's my mate. I know. Come."

Rahz draws back his shoulders. "There's no need to be so harsh. Give him a moment."

I'm frozen, tension roiling through every muscle. I have a death grip on Rahz's hand that must be painful, but he doesn't complain. While I sort out my thoughts, the others stare at me, my friends with patience and my father with barely contained irritation.

Could it be true? Is that why my mind is foggy as if waking from a dream? Because that's what's happening to Mother?

It makes sense. I'm beginning to believe it might be true, and with that belief comes an overwhelming rush of emotion, so strong as to slam me sideways.

Rahz catches me. "It's okay. Go. I know you have to go. Flying is faster, and I'll be right behind you on Magna. Go and meet your mother."

I stare up at him, never wishing he could fly more than I do right now. "Come with me."

"I am. I will. Go, Jinny. It's okay. I'll meet you there as soon as I can."

My body is in motion without the full participation of my mind, which is overwrought with yearning. I have only a moment to be grateful Father bothered to find me and tell me before he launches himself into the air, whether I follow or not.

I dart closer to Rahz for a quick kiss, spread my wings, and take off after Father. We fly to Clodhill as fast as our wings can carry us. The whole time, my thoughts are racing.

Mother, mother, mother.

At last, after all these years. But I'm supposed to leave Jodpirn soon. Tomorrow.

Well, I can't leave now, not when she's finally awake.

But Rahz! My heart wrenches in two, a painful pressure in my chest that makes it harder and harder to keep up with Father.

The night air is cool beneath my wings, but it fails to soothe me. Inside lives a turmoil of hope, fear, and vulnerability that ratchets that queasy feeling in my stomach up a notch.

Our arrival at the temple passes by in a blur. We wash our feet and change shoes in a rush of muscle memory, both eager to pass through the inner chamber to the transition rooms kept for dormant fae who've finally opened their eyes to the world once more.

A tendril of fear snakes up my spine.

What if I'm not good enough? What if she's disappointed in how I've turned out? What if she's cold, like Father, and all this time I've been waiting for nothing more than another heartache?

I don't know if I could bear it if that turned out to be true.

Father speaks with the guardians, who seem happy to see us. Happy to guide us to our recently awoken loved one.

The incense tickles my nose, and I hold in a sneeze. At least it gives me an excuse for my watery eyes.

Trailing in Father's wake down the marble steps, through a long, dimly lit hallway, and into an antechamber I've never seen before, I clench my throat to hold back nausea. I've never been so nervous, so excited, so everything. My skin prickles with sensation as though it's too much for my poor little body to hold inside.

"You're lucky. She's woken clear-headed and remembers much," the guardian is saying, glancing from Father to me and back. "She's waiting for you both. She's been asking for you."

My heart thuds wildly as we approach the threshold. The guardian lays a comforting hand on my shoulder as if sensing I need a little encouragement. I appreciate the gesture. It would have been nice if Father had thought to do it, but I'm glad to have the guardian's extra care.

Only a thin paneled wooden door separates me from the moment I've been waiting for my whole life.

Father knocks gently.

A sweet feminine voice calls out, "Come in."

A chill shivers its way from my head to my toes. I'm so excited I could burst.

Father pushes the door open and steps in first. The eternity wherein I'm stuck just behind him with no view of her ticks by at a snail's pace. My pulse swishes in my ears.

"Elara, my love," he says, a lightness in his tone that's brand new. He rushes to her bedside, where she sits atop the green satin cover, and I get my first look.

They embrace. Her purple hair, just a shade lighter than my own, spills in curls over his shoulder. Her skin is milky pale with a pink shimmer, also like mine, and her nails gleam white as if polished. The sparkling lights overhead cast a patchwork lattice over the two of them as they kiss.

Father's back is shaking as he holds her. Is he crying? I've never seen my father cry.

She lifts her head, and her warm honeyed-peach eyes catch mine. My bottom lip quivers. When she smiles, her cheeks plump, and her eyes crinkle at the corners. "Jindal?"

She's so beautiful. I nearly faint from forgetting to breathe. "Mother."

"My son." Her voice is music. Her smile is the sunshine itself, melting my heart into a warm gooey puddle. She lets go of Father and opens her arms to me.

All worry and fear evaporate as joy courses through my veins thicker than blood ever could be.

I collapse into her arms and hold on to her for dear life. "Momma."

Chapter Twenty-Two

R AHZ

W ATCHING THE TWO OF THEM TOGETHER WAS LIKE watching a spring fern unfurl in the morning sunshine. Jindal glowed under his mother's doting attention, and she warmed the room with her love.

I arrived as fast as I could, in time to meet her before night crept along and Jindal's father insisted we go to bed and leave them alone together.

All four of us will sleep in the temple tonight, Jindal's parents in her transition room and we in dormitory-style guest quarters I didn't realize the temple provided.

Though our little windowless room is sparse, it has everything we need: a wash basin, soap, fresh bathing cloths, a night pot, and a single bed we had to assure the guardian we'd make do. He'd offered us a second room, but no way am I leaving Jin all by himself tonight.

We'll just have to cuddle.

"How are you?" I push his hair behind his ears and cup his nape.

Jindal leans into my touch like he always does, but his eyes are filled to the brim with emotion, not all of it good.

"I don't know." He sucks his bottom lip into his mouth and bites. His hands tangle in the fabric of my tunic. "I'm...I'm happy, and the ache in my soul that's yearned for Momma all these years is all healed up, but I'm also...I'm also..."

"It's all right if you don't have words for it."

"Torn," he lets out with an unsettled moan. "We're supposed to leave in the morning, but, well, I can't leave now, can I?"

Those words I expected but didn't want to hear. It's as if the ache in his soul has been transferred to mine.

My heart is heavy with guilt. My first thought upon hearing Jindal's mother had emerged from dormancy was happiness for him. But my second? My second thought was, *oh no. Now he won't come with me. We'll be torn apart after all.* And it's no good to be feeling sorry for myself when this should be one of the best days of my lover's life.

I won't deny the part of my mind that wishes he'd choose me, but I'll never, ever say it out loud. I won't put him in the terrible position of picking between me and his mother. He'll always have us both, even if we're separated for a time. But I'm devastated to leave him behind. Especially when I thought he'd be with me.

I rub his shoulders, massaging out the tension he holds there. "I won't leave in the morning. It can wait one more day. Let's not think of it now."

He gives a sad little nod. "Thank you. For waiting."

We're silent as we strip off our clothes and prepare for bed. Silent as we use the little basin to wash one another up. Silent as we climb under the blankets and burrow into each other.

I hold him close, his soft wings against my chest, me

cocooned around him like a shell protecting its pearl. His steady heartbeat is a comfort, even as my thoughts race. Delaying a day will mean pushing Magna harder to make up the time. But she's so strong now, so fit for this type of travel, I'm confident she'll take to the change with ease.

When Jindal's voice breaks through my fretting, it's so quiet I hardly hear him. "Do you think Father will be...any different? Now that she's awake?"

Ah, he is worrying about that as well. I should have known. "How do you mean?"

"More kind? More loving?" He shifts in my arms, scooting back as far as possible into my embrace. "Or am I being silly just for thinking it?"

"Not silly, no." I kiss his soft hair. "It's fair to think of what might be, but maybe don't get your hopes up." I can't imagine Jindal's father changing, and even if he does, I'll never fully forgive him for how he's treated Jin all these years. As if he's not enough, not worthy, not lovable. When he is all those things and more. Any father would be lucky to have such a son.

"It'll be different. Having two parents at home." He tenses. "Oh, Rahz. What of Bessa? Father won't need her anymore if Mother is home."

"Aww, Bessa will always be our family. She's going to be so happy for you."

"But what will she do now?"

"What she's always done. She'll love you, she'll bake, she'll cook, and she'll live her life as she sees fit. Her talents are well known throughout Jodpirn. Many will be delighted to trade with her. Don't worry. Bessa can take care of herself without your father's coin."

He lets out a big sigh, and his body relaxes a fraction. "You're right. Of course you are. I should've known that if I'd been thinking clearly."

"I don't know you're meant to be thinking clearly after such a momentous evening. Don't be so hard on yourself."

"You always know just what to say." He laces his fingers with mine, our hands resting over his belly as it rises and falls. He squeezes. "I don't know what I'll do without you."

Come with me, my heart pleads, but I refuse to make this harder on him than it already is.

I close my eyes and take comfort in the feel of him against me, the familiar lilac scent of his hair, and the way he squirms as he finds the best position to fall asleep in, our bodies touching from head to toe.

The room is quiet. The temple sleeps for the night. Tomorrow we'll take Elara home and get her settled back in Jodpirn.

I'm drifting off as Jindal shivers and sniffles.

"I don't want you to go." His voice sounds as if he's about to cry.

His words hit like a knife to the chest. How can I leave him now? When he's feeling so fragile. So vulnerable. What kind of partner am I if I abandon him at this pivotal moment in his life?

"Oh, Jin." I bury my face in his hair.

But what of all those people down south? Hundreds? Thousands? Innocent women and children are on the slaughtering block because Aurielle's tyranny demands everyone pay for the rebellion of few. What of them? Will Suvi's troops be enough to save them without my magic?

They need me too. They need me to hide them while the conflict gets sorted. To help keep them safe. I can't abandon them either.

Do I put the well-being of one ahead of the lives of many? Even if he's the one I love most in the entire realm? It seems terribly selfish.

"Rahz?" Jindal turns in my arms and studies my face. It's

dark, but his eyesight is better than mine. Whatever he sees startles a little gasp from his lips.

"Oh, Rahz. I'm sorry. I shouldn't have said that." He kisses me. "Of course you have to go. And I understand. I do. I'm just a mess right now. Ignore me."

"That, I could never do, my love. Never." I return the kiss. A sweet press of lips which neither of us deepens. Being skin to skin like this is enough. Holding each other, perhaps for the last time in a long time.

I'd always imagined the day Jindal's mother awoke would be a happy one, full of rejoicing. I never thought we would be caught up in so much turmoil. This isn't how it should be. It's not fair to either of them.

But when has life ever been fair?

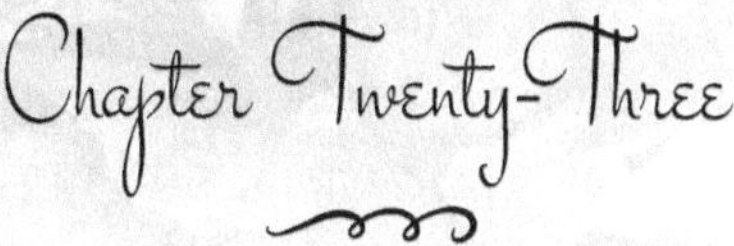

Chapter Twenty-Three

Jindal

As we stroll through our garden toward the thriving fields, Mother takes my hand. Her skin is soft and warm against mine. We are of the same height, shoulder to shoulder, both of us basking in the sunlight on our faces.

It's early afternoon. We made the trip home this morning, Mother and Rahz on horseback with Father and I flying above. She'll need some time to regain her full strength, but she looks good next to me, healthy and vibrant. One day we'll go flying together. Though it might be a ways away, I can't wait.

We walk in companionable silence until we're beyond the back gate and well out of earshot of the house.

She says, "I wanted to have some time alone with you, Jindal. We have much to discuss."

Do we? I mean, I suppose we do. We have *everything* to discuss, really, but her tone holds a hint of hesitancy. I get the feeling she's thinking of something specific.

Being with her is both wonderful and oddly nerve-racking.

In one way, I feel as if I've known her forever. This is my mother, and I've visited her often. I've confided many things to her over the years. How much she remembers, I have no idea, but we aren't strangers, she and I.

And yet we are. Because in another way, I'm worried about how one-sided our relationship feels. It never occurred to me, as I poured my secrets out to her sleeping form, that I knew next to nothing of her in return.

She knows my every fear, my every hope, my every failing and success. And all I know about her is that we look alike.

I try to sound calmer than I feel. "What did you want to talk about?"

"So many things." She turns her brilliant smile on me, which helps to settle my nerves a bit. "But first, your father."

Just kidding, my nerves are back and rattled. "What about him?" It's harder to keep my voice at an even keel when thinking about my father.

She squeezes my hand. "Oh, darling. I remember your visits."

"You do?" A swooping sensation tumbles through me. All that talking. *She remembers.* My mother *knows* me. I could weep with joy.

"Yes, especially when you were younger and hadn't yet thought to censor your feelings in order to spare mine. Not word for word, mind you, never like that, but I remember your longing to please him. Your sorrow at feeling like you didn't. His coldness toward you. It broke my heart."

"I'm sorry. I never meant to—"

"Shh, I know. I know. I'm glad you came to me. I wish I'd been able to wake for you." She stops us walking and turns me to face her. "I wish I hadn't fallen dormant when you were born. It will be my life's greatest sadness. But we're together now, and I would help mend the rift between you and your father if it's in my power."

Her words mean the world to me, but I can't bring myself to tell her the damage has already been done. I don't know I want to mend the rift with Father. Lately, we leave each other alone for the most part, and it's the most peace I've ever had in the relationship. I'd prefer it to continue. Sure, it would be great if he were nicer, but that alone won't mend the rift.

My mouth hangs open as my thoughts fly by, but I don't know what to say.

She cups my cheek. "He wasn't always like this, you know? He was good once. I don't know what happened when I fell dormant, but it's not your fault. I love you enough for both of us, and I'm so, *so* proud of you, my son."

I might faint. My knees shiver and threaten to buckle. My lips quiver. A rush of warmth fills my chest, and tears form in my eyes. To know she's proud means so much to me.

"Come here." She folds her arms around my shoulders, protecting me from such big feelings.

I hug her waist. "I missed you so much. I never knew you, but I missed you with my whole heart."

"Yes, I know what that feels like." We rock together. "I missed you with my whole heart as well. I missed your first word, your first steps, and your every first since then. But you know what I do remember?"

"What's that?"

"Your first kiss."

"What?"

I lean back to look at her, at the teasing grin splitting her face and the light in her eyes. "You were so excited to tell me you'd finally kissed your Rahz. The joy bubbled out in your every word. Of all your visits, that's perhaps the one I remember most vividly."

Heat creeps across my cheeks. "It was a very good kiss."

"A very good hour or two of kisses if what you said was true."

Somehow I'm giggling and crying at once. Happy tears. "I can't believe you remember that."

"That was around the time you stopped fearing the Gatekeeper because nothing could harm you so long as you had Rahz. I was happy for you then."

Those old childhood fears seem so silly now. "But I don't know anything about you."

"You have only to ask. For you, I'm an open book."

There's so much I want to know. So much I've always wanted to know. Perhaps the most burning questions are why Father? What did you ever see in him? But I'm not sure it's time for that conversation, though it does feel good to know I can ask when I'm ready.

"We have the gift of time," she says, probably to stop my thoughts from racing so much. "Time for me to sort out your father. To find out why he's changed and to help him remember the man he used to be. Time to spend with you, my son, and make up for what we lost. Time to thank Bessa for everything she's done for me. For *you*. Time to get to know your sweet, handsome Rahz."

My breath catches in my throat. She doesn't know he's leaving.

And as hard as it will be to say good-bye to my mother so soon, I'm not sure I can let him leave without me.

Her eyes blaze. "Oh, dear. What is it? What's wrong?"

I shake my head. If only I were better with words in the moment, but my tongue is always stubborn when I need it the most.

"Is it something I've said?" Her expression is so full of concern. The way Rahz looks at me sometimes when I'm upset. A look I've never received from my father.

"No, no, it's not you. It's Rahz. I have something to tell you. And Father as well." No matter how much I dread the conversation.

"Shall I call to him?"

"You can do that?"

"He's my mate. Of course I can."

I blink, stunned. "Can Rahz and I do that?"

"I don't see why not. I'm surprised you haven't learned."

"Will you teach us?"

"Yes. But let me get your father here so you can say what's on your mind."

A roiling wave of nausea threatens to overtake me, but I nod. I have to face him. And I have to face myself, to learn to be true to my own sense of right and wrong, however slow it was to come to me.

Mother wraps an arm around my waist as we wait. It doesn't take long before his silhouette turns up in the sky, wings flapping furiously to get to us. One little call from her and he comes racing. What power she has.

He's been a different person these last dozen hours. So attentive to her every need. Smiling like I've never seen. Voice warm and calm. He must have missed her terribly, even if he never showed the emotion. But what I don't understand is why he never did. It would have been one thing we had in common. Maybe we could have bonded...

I shake off this line of thinking. What-ifs have never done me any good.

He lands with a whoosh of air and a graceful lunge, gray wings folding neatly on his back. "What is it, Elara? Are you all right?" His gaze passes over both of us and lingers on me. I must look as nervous as I feel.

"We're both fine. We'd like you to join us on our walkabout," she says, letting me off the hook if I need it. No pressure to say anything in particular. That helps.

"I'd love that." He gestures to the field up ahead. "I can show you this year's crop. So many beans, more than we can ever eat."

"That's good." She takes his arm, and we walk. The movement helps too.

The two of them chitchat as I work up my nerve. Already I see the beginnings of the partner in my mother that I've always longed for. Someone to listen to my side when interacting with Father while he's being difficult. A parent who supports me and wants me to be happy. Someone I can support in return. I get the sense she could go on like this all day, covering for me as I muster up the courage to broach an important subject with them.

I clear my throat, and two sets of eyes turn my way. Now or never.

"Mother, Father, Rahz has been called into royal service in the south. In Irondale." I waver. Do I mention who for? If I don't, they'll assume Aurielle. If I do, and they disagree with Suvi's interference in her mother's plans, I risk the mission. I stay silent on that point. Better to keep it to myself for now. "He's expected within the coming weeks and must leave at once."

Mother's face morphs to concern, while Father's—I can't read him. That he isn't immediately angry I'll take as a win.

"Oh darling, how long will he be gone?"

"I don't know. But he asked me to go with him, and I said yes. I gave it a lot of thought first. It felt wrong to leave while you were sleeping. It will be even harder now that you're awake. I want to be with you very badly, but Rahz is my mate. I love him. We belong together."

Father scowls. So much for him not being angry. "You can't go. I need your help on the farm, and I won't allow you to leave your mother now. Look at her. You're hurting her feelings."

I swallow and shift my gaze.

But Mother holds up her hand as if in protest. "No, no. He's right. If Rahz must go, then so must Jindal. He hasn't hurt my feelings. I'm only sad our reunion must wait a bit longer, that's all."

Unwavering support. Oh, how I've yearned for her. How hard will it be to leave her when she's everything I've always wanted?

"Elara, the crops. Who will help come harvest if Jindal is off gallivanting across the country?"

"I will, of course."

"You need to rest."

"I've rested enough. My strength is returning. In no time I'll be back to my old self, and I'm looking forward to farming again. We'll make do without Jinny."

My nickname from her lips brings a smile to my face. Father never calls me Jinny. But my friends do. Rahz does. And now, so does my mother. "Rahz has enlisted Vander to coordinate volunteers to keep up with my work while I'm away."

"Vander." Father scoffs. "That moron? Why him? You don't even like him."

So Father knows a little something about me after all. "It won't just be him taking shifts. Others will help. Our friends. But Vander's family is good at scheduling staff."

Before he can complain further, Mother speaks. "I'll look forward to meeting your friends and to getting to know you through them while you're away. But, son, tell us, Rahz has been called into service for what? What's he tasked to do?"

This I must balance delicately. "Do you remember my last visit?"

"A bit, though it's fuzzy."

"There's been some trouble in Irondale between humans and fae. Who better than mixlings to help them iron out their differences? The goal is to restore the peace, the safety of the people, and the trade routes."

"So much has happened while I slumbered."

Yes. My entire life. Rahz's as well. "You're really all right with me leaving?" I look at her, not father, who's still scowling but has enough sense to stay quiet.

"I'll miss you, but you explained yourself quite well. You must follow your heart, and your heart is with Rahz."

"And with you."

"And me." She smiles. "I shall look forward to your return."

We haven't even left yet, and already I look forward to our return. Perhaps, in that time, she'll talk some sense into Father.

Chapter Twenty-Four

RAHZ

My bags are already packed. They were never completely unpacked, but I'm picking through them again anyway. Maybe I forgot something.

Maybe there's something here I still need.

I'm fidgety, restless, and without anything useful to do. All that's left is to leave, but I promised Jin I'd wait until tomorrow morning.

Though I'd like to be spending this time with him, our last day corresponds with his first day back with his mother. It's only fair to give them some privacy, so I came to be with my mum while I wait.

"Do you have anything that needs mending before you go? That would keep our hands busy," she says from the rocking chair in the corner.

We're in our main room, and I can't help but feel like I'm keeping her from whatever work she would be doing if I wasn't still lingering. When I showed up with the story of Jindal's mother finally waking, we'd already said our good-byes, and that leaves us in this liminal space, unsure of what to do with ourselves.

"Actually, yes. That's a good idea." I dig through the bag I have open and pull out a couple of my older shirts. "Would you prefer the one with the hole at the elbow or the torn seam at the cuff?"

"Seam, please. You can patch the hole."

"Deal." I hand her the shirt and fetch our sewing supplies. "And thank you."

"My pleasure." She probably even means it. Mum is good with a needle and thread. I'm merely passable, but it'll do to mend a hole.

We settle in again, each with our project, both of us quiet. Waiting has never been in either of our skill sets. We prefer doing. And I'm too sad to put effort into a cheerful conversation when all I feel is dread over my and Jindal's inevitable parting.

Mum, as if reading my mind, says, "It won't be forever. You'll be back before you know it, and the two of you will pick up right where you left off."

She's right, but her words do nothing to ease the ache in my chest. "I don't want to say good-bye to him. Not again. It was hard enough when I was only going to be gone for a month, but now? Who knows how long this mission will take?"

She hums, drawing needle and thread through fabric with care. "You could stay. Princess Suvi is fae. Surely, she'll understand the importance of one's mother waking from dormancy."

"I've thought about backing out. But if I stay and word comes that the humans of Irondale have all been slaughtered by the queen's troops, I'll never be able to forgive myself. I have to do this."

"You're a good man, Rahz, with a good heart. I'm lucky to be your mother, and Jindal is lucky to be your mate. Trust he knows that and will wait for you with open arms."

"Oh, Mum." I release a big sigh and resolve not to cry. "I wish he were coming with me. I'll be so lonely. And so worried about him while I'm away. I thought, well, even after his mother woke, I'd hoped maybe he'd still choose me." My shoulders sink. "But I know he couldn't."

"Listen." She sets her sewing on her lap and tilts up my chin. "It isn't about him choosing his mother over you any more than it's about you choosing Princess Suvi over him. That's not what's happening. It's about both of you following the paths you need to follow, even if they diverge for some time. Those sorts of decisions won't always be easy or clear, but you must be true to yourselves."

A breath shudders out of me. "You always know what to say."

"But it hasn't made you feel any better."

No, it hasn't, but... "It's good to hear nonetheless."

"I'm sorry I can't fix this for you."

I miss those days when I was small and Mum could fix everything that went sideways in my world with nothing more than a kind word, a warm embrace, and a kiss on my forehead. But those days are long gone.

Three loud thumps wring a startled jolt out of both of us.

"Rahz! Ms. Starling! It's Jinny. Can I come in?"

From the excitement in his voice, I'm surprised he didn't bash the door down.

Mum calls out, "Of course, dear. Door's unlocked."

A vibrating person-shaped bundle of energy whooshes into our living room in a flutter of shimmering wings and untamed purple hair. He's got bags hanging off both shoulders, preventing him from settling his wings properly. He promptly dumps them in the middle of the floor and leaps at me from across the room.

I rush to get the sewing needle out of pricking range while he squeals, "I'm coming with you. Again. Were you worried? I'm sorry. I was confused about what I should do, but my home is wherever you are. So I'm coming with you."

His lips are on mine before I've properly heard his words. Coming with me? After all? A cresting rush of joy overtakes me, and my heart skips a beat. Or four. "Really?"

"Yes. I've already spoken to Mother and Father, and they understand. Well, she understands and insists she'll handle him from here."

Relief swells in my chest. I feel like a man who's been caught in a whirlpool, circling wildly from delight to despair, and finally, someone has thrown me a raft. My head is above water, and everything is going to be all right after all. I'm so happy, it's hard to catch my breath.

Jin goes on, chattering away in that excited voice I love so much. "I'm already packed, and I brought my bags, so we can go now if you like. You said you could delay for me, but you also said the timing is crucial, so I thought I'd come ready to leave. Where's Briar? With Magna? Thank you for taking care of them so I could talk to Momma."

While he talks a mile a minute, Mum and I exchange meaningful glances. Her warm brown eyes crinkle at the corners. She's happy for me, and I'm so grateful for both of them I could weep. Instead, I kiss Jin and slide him from my lap to the spot next to me.

"Yes, Briar's in the stables with Magna. We can leave as soon as I finish this." I hold up the needle and retrieve my sewing project from where it's landed on the floor. "I can't believe you're coming with me."

A bright smile lights his face. "I can't believe I almost didn't. I'm just thankful I realized what I needed to do before you left and I have to come chasing after you."

Mum speaks up. "I don't suppose you have any mending that needs doing while Rahz finishes?" She tosses me my shirt, cuff seam back intact, and raises her brows at Jindal.

His cheeks pinken. "Well, now that you mention it."

Mother huffs. "Hand it over, lad. Let's get you boys set up properly for your adventure."

While Jindal rifles through his bag and retrieves a small pile of clothes, I think on her words. *Adventure.* That's not how I've been looking at this mission, but with Jindal at my side and a little bit of luck, she might be right.

We can help people who need it and make an adventure out of the mission at the same time. We'll be traversing more than half of Luminia on this journey, more of the realm than many will see in their lifetime. And we'll be doing it together.

Jindal leans into my side, making it more difficult to sew, but I don't mind. We belong side by side. There's nothing we can't face as long as we're together.

And we'll be together always.

BE ASSURED, DEAR READER, THAT RAHZ AND JINDAL live happily ever after. But if you'd like a sneak peek into their adventures (and an extra spicy scene!), I've written a free bonus story for you that didn't quite fit in the novel. It's here: https://dl.bookfunnel.com/7nlmhz32rb

AND IF YOU'VE ENJOYED THIS INTRODUCTION TO MY Luminia Realm, there's more to come. Gatherdawn: Luminia Volume I, Gatherdusk: Luminia Volume II, and The Gatekeeper: A Luminia Novel are headed your way soon!

HAPPY READING!
~Lee

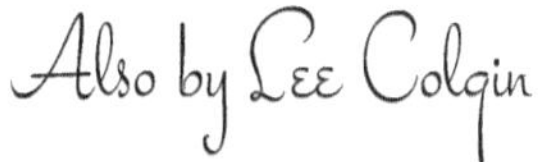

Mongrel

~A misfit werewolf

~A guilt-ridden vampire

A chilling mystery!

Changeling

~A dominant incubus who hates faeries

~A faerie with a crush on the grumpy incubus

Forced together as trespassers infiltrate the territory, will enemies become lovers or will a curse keep them apart forever?

Stray

~A grumpy were-panther stuck in his ways

~A young vampire with a troubles past

A love story neither of them expected.

Beneath the Opal Arc

~A rare male witch who saves the world

~The vampire who saves him

In a race to safety will love flourish or will war tear them apart?

Across the Sapphire Sea

~A possessive lover bent on discovering a hidden cure

~A feisty fledgling eager for a hint of independence

Can their love last or will ancient secrets shatter their bond forever?

Beyond the Ruby River

~An Ancient Egyptian leading a simple Life

~A demon half-breed, his incubus lover

Will their love last forever or is each soul destined to pine for the other for eternity?

Over the Emerald Valley

~A clever concubine

~A dutiful army general

The mystery of the missing emeralds!

Slay My Love

~A sweet talking vampire

~A duty-bound slayer

Will love triumph or will one have to kill the other to survive?

Feral Dawn

~A lone werewolf

~An injured vampire left for dead

Can a disgraced vampire & an outcast wolf find love,

or will the ghosts of their pasts divide them?

M.M. Scrooge

A very naughty MM retelling of the classic, *A Christmas Carol*

A Bridge to a Troll's Heart

When a lonely bridge troll meets a cheerful wolf shifter, will he leave his precious bridge for a chance at love? Find out in this grumpy/sunshine, friends-to-lovers, found family romance today!

Forbidden Devotion

(Paranormal Hunger Book I)

~A vampire heir at a werewolf university

~An alpha wolf who hates vampires

Will love conquer all—or is war inevitable?

Forbidden Flirtation

(Paranormal Hunger Book II)

~An esteemed vampire surgeon

~A young, injured werewolf

Can love flourish between enemy species despite a society in turmoil?

Forbidden Obsession

(Paranormal Hunger Book III)

~A jaded vampire too damaged for love

~A lovesick shifter who refuses to give up

Will destiny unite them—or will old enemies reign?

About the Author

Lee Colgin has loved vampires since she read *Dracula* on a hot sunny beach at 13 years old. She lives in North Carolina with lots of dogs and her husband. No, he's not a vampire, but she loves him anyway. Lee likes cookies and pizza.

Email: LeeColgin@gmail.com
Website: www.leecolgin.com

facebook.com/authorleecolgin

twitter.com/leecolgin

instagram.com/authorleecolgin

amazon.com/author/leecolgin

bookbub.com/profile/lee-colgin

tiktok.com/@authorleecolgin